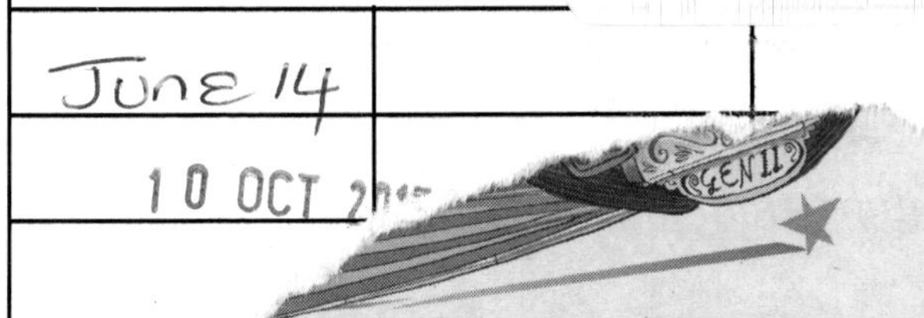

… Cottrell Boyce's books are loved …d the world by readers of all ages. They … won or been shortlisted for every major UK …ward. His first novel, *Millions*, was made into a feature film. His second, *Framed*, was adapted for BBC television. His third book, *Cosmic*, is currently being developed for cinema. Frank is also a successful screenwriter and helped to create the unforgettable Opening Ceremony for the London 2012 Olympic Games.

Joe Berger is a much-loved children's author, illustrator and cartoonist. He makes prize-winning animated short films and is co-creator of the food cartoon in the *Guardian* magazine each Saturday. He has also been an official illustrator for World Book Day. Joe lives in Bristol with his wife and three children.

Other cracking

Chitty Chitty Bang Bang

adventures from Macmillan Children's Books

By Ian Fleming

Chitty Chitty Bang Bang

By Frank Cottrell Boyce

Chitty Chitty Bang Bang Flies Again

Chitty Chitty Bang Bang
and the Race Against Time

Frank Cottrell Boyce

Chitty Chitty BANG BANG
OVER THE MOON

Illustrated
by Joe Berger

MACMILLAN CHILDREN'S BOOKS

Chitty Chitty Bang Bang Over the Moon
is approved by the Ian Fleming Estate.

First published 2013 by Macmillan Children's Books

This edition published 2014 by Macmillan Children's Books
a division of Macmillan Publishers Limited
20 New Wharf Road, London N1 9RR
Basingstoke and Oxford
Associated companies throughout the world
www.panmacmillan.com

ISBN 978-0-330-54421-4

1 3 5 7 9 8 6 4 2

A CIP catalogue record for this book is available from
the British Library.

Printed and bound by CPI Group (UK) Ltd, Croydon CR0 4YY

For Joe and Phyllis as they set out
on their great adventure

1

Most cars are just cars. Four wheels. An engine. Some seats. They take you to work or to school or on holiday. They bring you home again.

But the Tooting family didn't have a car.

The Tooting family were Mum, Dad, Jem and Lucy and the baby – Little Harry. They used to have the most beautiful car in the world – a perfectly restored Paragon Panther called Chitty Chitty Bang Bang. She had silver wheels that flashed in the sunshine. Her seats were soft as silk. Under her long

golden bonnet was an engine so powerful that she could fly, not just through the air, but through time itself. In her, the Tootings had travelled through the dinosaur swamps of prehistoric Earth. They had seen the Ice Age come and go. They had partied in jazz-age New York and looked upon El Dorado, the fabulous lost city of gold.

But now Chitty Chitty Bang Bang had been stolen.

If an ordinary family car is stolen, its owners might have to walk home, or wait for the bus. When Chitty Chitty Bang Bang was stolen, the Tootings were stranded where no bus could help them.

They were stranded . . .

. . . in the past.

In London in 1966, to be precise.

Just outside Wembley Stadium on 30 July at ten minutes to three, to be very precise indeed.

'Everyone stay calm,' said Jem. 'I have a plan to get us out of here and back to our own time.'

'Not now, Jem,' said Mum.

'Not now?! What do you mean, not now? We're stuck in a time fifty years before we were born. Meanwhile in our own time Tiny Jack – the greatest thief in history – has got his hands on Chitty Chitty Bang Bang – the greatest car in history. Imagine what he could steal with Chitty as his getaway vehicle. He could go back in time and steal all the gold in El Dorado. He could steal the *Mona Lisa* while the paint is still wet. He will be the richest and most powerful person on Earth. Imagine that – a planet ruled by evil supervillain Tiny Jack!'

'Jem,' said Mum, 'do you realize what's about to happen in this stadium? Only the most important game of football ever played, that's all. Tell him, Dad.'

'The word today,' said Dad, 'is *World Cup Final, 1966*. England win four–two, thanks to a hat-trick from Geoff Hurst. The only time England have ever won the World Cup. The greatest day in the entire history of our nation, and we are going to see it!' He squeezed Mum's hand and pulled her towards the queue of flag-waving supporters who were filing through the turnstiles.

'We can't watch the match – we've got to get back to our own time!'

'After the match,' said Dad.

'Enjoy the moment,' said Mum. 'It's 1966! It's not just the World Cup Final. It's swinging London, miniskirts, the Beatles.'

Dad surveyed the scene – the football fans with their brightly coloured rosettes and wooden rattles covered in ribbons; the old men in flat caps; the young men in long fur coats and top hats, some in strange antique army uniforms. There were girls in tiny dresses – some covered in black and white zigzags, others with orange flowers, one with mirrors.

'People are staring at us,' muttered Lucy. 'They think our clothes are weird.'

'They're not weird,' said Mum. 'Just a bit ahead of their time.'

'Look at these cars,' sighed Dad. 'MGs, Rovers, Rolls-Royces, Jaguars, Triumphs . . . I don't know about the rest of you, but I could live like this.'

'And I would rather,' said Lucy, 'freeze to death in the Ice Age and be eaten by a mammoth that thought I was an ice lolly, than wear a miniskirt.'

By now they had reached the turnstiles. 'Tickets please,' said the man in the kiosk.

'Tickets?' Dad gasped. 'We don't have any tickets!'

'Tickets!' Mum wailed. 'What will we do?'

'No tickets, no entrance,' said the man in the booth. 'Step aside, please, and let legitimate ticket holders pass.'

The children followed Mum and Dad as they moped back into the street. 'What will we do now?' said Mum.

'Save the world?' suggested Jem. 'I do have a plan. You see, Commander Pott, the man who first restored Chitty Chitty Bang Bang—'

'Commander Caractacus Pott is a very busy man,' said Dad. 'He's probably busy doing secret work of national importance. We couldn't disturb him. Let's just enjoy the match.'

'That's just it, he's here at the match. We saw him. All we have to do is . . .'

'Psssst.' A man in a Union Jack bowler hat was hissing at them from behind a lamp post. 'Wanna buy a ticket?'

'We certainly do,' said Mum. 'We want five.'

'Only got two.'

'Oh,' said Mum. 'Never mind. Lucy and I will watch the match. Dad can look after Jem and Little Harry.'

'Or a better idea,' said Dad. 'Jem and I will go to the match and you look after Lucy and Little Harry.'

'Or what about—'

'If it's no trouble,' interrupted the bowler-hat man, 'could we settle the money matters first and your family problems later? It's two guineas per ticket.'

'Two guineas!' said Mum. 'That's two pounds and ten pence. That's so cheap!'

'Two guineas each, mind,' said the man.

In 1966 £4.20 was a lot of money, but to Mum and Dad it sounded like next to nothing. Last time they'd gone to a football match they'd paid ten times that, and England hadn't even won the World Cup! Their chests swelled at the thought that suddenly they were rich. If £4.20 could buy you two tickets for the World Cup Final, then the twenty-pound note in Mum's purse was probably enough for a luxury family holiday.

'Honestly,' said Dad, 'we'll give you twice that. More. Here's a tenner.'

He whipped a ten-pound note out of his pocket while the man slid a pair of World Cup Final tickets out from under the crown of his bowler. But when he caught sight of Dad's money the man snarled, 'What do you call that?'

'I call it a ten-pound note,' said Dad. 'Keep the change.'

'A ten-pound note?!' said the man. 'Why, it's hardly bigger than a postage stamp. Who's this hairy geezer on the back?'

'That is Charles Darwin!'

'Charles Darwin?! Where's Her Majesty the Queen?'

'Here on the front, look.'

'That big old boiler? That's not Her Majesty. Her Majesty's a slip of a girl. That is not a tenner.'

'It certainly is,' says Dad. 'Look, it says so.'

'Saying so doesn't mean it is so. I've got a parrot can say so. That doesn't make it legal tender. A parrot's a parrot and money is money. This –' he pulled out a piece of paper the size of a tablecloth, decorated with a picture of the Queen as a pretty young woman – 'is money. And that –' he pointed to Dad's banknote – 'is a very small portrait of a Victorian scientist. That's all. I'm not swapping World Cup Final tickets for that. You must be mad.'

Dad was frantic. He had to have those tickets. He rummaged through his wallet. 'Would you take a credit card?' He held out his credit card for the man to see.

The man gave the small square of blue plastic a look so withering that Jem was amazed the card didn't curl up from pure shame. 'Oh, of course I'll take that,' he smirked. 'Why, of course I will. The moment I got a hold of these tickets for the most important game of football ever played, I thought to myself: I wonder will anyone ever swap them for a small piece of plastic such as I can pick my teeth with or use as a bookmark? That was my dream, but I never dared hope that my dream would come true.'

Dad looked hopeful until Lucy whispered, 'Just to be clear, Dad, he's being sarcastic.'

'Oh,' said Dad. 'That's a pity.'

'What about a cash machine?' said Mum.

'Oh, a cash machine?' said the man.

'You know, a hole in the wall. Cash comes out of it.'

'A hole in the wall that cash comes out of? Yes, of course, there's lots of them over there just behind the money bushes. See where the road is paved with gold?'

Mum looked where the man was pointing, but then Jem whispered to her, 'He's being sarcastic again. We're in 1966. Cash machines aren't invented yet.'

Mum was rooting in the bottom of her handbag. 'Look!' she whooped. 'Gold! Real gold! We got it in El Dorado.' She scraped a few curls and scraps of gold out from the lining of her bag with her fingernails and opened her hand so the man could see the little heap of shiny shavings in the middle of her palm. 'There must be a hundred pounds' worth there at least,' she said. 'Surely you'd swap the tickets for real gold?'

'I'll swap them for two guineas each,' he said. 'No more. No less. Now move along and stop wasting my time. I've half a mind to go to the coppers and tell them about those forged banknotes of yours.'

'They're not forged,' said Dad, stuffing the

money back in his wallet. 'They're just a bit ahead of their time.'

But Mum and Dad did move off, just in case.

'We need to find Commander Pott and his family,' said Jem. 'We need to explain that we are from the future and that in the future their car – Chitty Chitty Bang Bang – has fallen into the hands of an evil genius who is planning to use it to—'

'Maybe we could shin up a drainpipe!' said Mum.

'What?'

'Or find an old fire escape? There must be some way to see this game.'

There was a terrible groan from inside the stadium. 'Germany's first goal,' said Mum. 'A header from Helmut Haller. That means we've missed twelve minutes already.'

'The word today,' said Dad, 'is *five goals to go*. We must not despair.'

'Are you listening to me?' asked Jem. But Mum and Dad were staring at the tall white impenetrable walls of the stadium. They seemed to think that if they just stared hard enough they would be able to see the match.

'Chitty Chitty Bang Bang!' yelled Little Harry.

'Yes,' said Jem. 'That's what we really need. We need Chitty back.' The truth was that Jem missed Chitty – the smell of her seats, the dazzle of her wheels, the music of her engines, the noise of her Klaxon – more than he missed his home in Zborowski Terrace, Basildon. As long as Chitty was with them, he didn't really care where in the world or when in history they were.

'Chitty Chitty Bang Bang!' insisted Little Harry.

'I know,' sighed Jem. 'How could she let herself be stolen like that?' For the truth was it seemed to Jem that Chitty never did anything she didn't want to do. She would never start on a cold morning unless you gave her vintage champagne, and no matter how carefully you planned your journey, you always somehow ended up not where you had intended to go, but where Chitty wanted to be. Deep inside Jem suspected that Chitty could only be stolen if she wanted to be stolen. Could she have just got bored of the Tooting family?

By now Mum and Dad had found a newspaper seller who had a transistor radio. They huddled around him, listening to the match. Jem and Lucy sat forlornly on the edge of the kerb while Little Harry played in the gutter.

'Chitty,' yelled Little Harry. 'Chitty,' he shouted. 'Bang!' He tugged at Jem's sleeve. 'Bang!'

Something about the way Little Harry was tugging his sleeve reminded Jem of this very important fact:

Little Harry is never wrong.

Which reminded him in turn of the absolutely important Little Harry Rule, which is . . .

Never ignore Little Harry.

Jem let Little Harry tug him across the pavement, past the hot-dog sellers. Lucy trudged after them. From here they could see a line of parked cars. Jem gasped. Lucy smiled. For there – parked neatly in a side road just to one side of the stadium entrance – was a car. And what a car. A twelve-cylinder, twenty-three-litre racing-green Paragon Panther with brand-new red leather upholstery and a cream-coloured collapsible roof. The afternoon sunshine blazed from her huge silver exhausts, and

the polished chrome of her snarling boa-constrictor horn glowed.

'It can't be,' said Lucy. 'It can't be Chitty, just standing there.'

'I knew she wouldn't let us down,' said Jem with a smile, not particularly truthfully. He half expected that twenty-three-litre engine to roar a welcome as they drew near. Maybe Chitty would fling open her doors or flash her headlights in greeting. She didn't. But that didn't matter. Jem was happy enough for both of them. He just wasn't sure how to say so. If Chitty had been human, there would have been hugs and handshakes, but those don't really work on cars. How do you greet a long-lost car? Do you pat her on the bonnet? Shake her by the gearstick? Perched on top of Chitty's radiator was her famous mascot – the Zborowski Lightning – a little model

of an aeroplane. Jem sometimes thought that flicking the propellers of the little plane was a bit like tickling her under the chin. He flicked them now. Then he whispered 'Good to see you, Chitty' into the radiator.

'GA GOOO GA!' Chitty Chitty Bang Bang sounded her Klaxon so loudly and fiercely that Jem's brain went numb. 'Ow! What did you do that for?' In the past he had heard Chitty blast her cry at dinosaurs, gangsters and traffic wardens, but never at him. They were supposed to be friends! What was going on? 'Chitty,' he said, bending down to the radiator again, 'don't you know me? It's me. Jem.'

'Ga gooo ga!' Chitty's Klaxon spat thunder into Jem's ear again.

By now people were beginning to look over, to see the cause of the disturbance.

'If you keep this up, you'll get us arrested,' said Lucy.

'Why doesn't she recognize us? Is it not the right Chitty?'

''Nother Chitty!' said Little Harry. ''Nother Chitty.'

'Of course it's not another Chitty,' said Jem, ignoring the Little Harry Rule. 'There is only one Chitty Chitty Bang Bang. The only Paragon Panther ever built.'

'Except,' said Lucy, 'last time we saw her she was gold, and now she's green.'

'Don't be so superficial,' said Jem. 'Colour doesn't matter. It's what's inside that counts.' It was true – inside they could see all the familiar controls – the button that made her into a submarine, the handle that made the parasols go up on sunny days and – most important of all – the Chronojuster dial, which allowed her to travel through time. There was definitely only one car that could travel through the air and under the sea and through the fabric of time itself. This was their own dear Chitty Chitty Bang Bang, but . . .

'This' said Lucy, 'is Chitty Chitty Bang Bang, 1966. This is Chitty Chitty Bang Bang before she ever met us, when she belonged to the Pott family. This Chitty Chitty Bang Bang doesn't know who we are.'

Jem stared at Chitty. Everything about her was familiar. Everything about her reminded him of the fabulous adventures they'd had together in jungles and deserts. It was sad and strange that she didn't remember him – as though he had met his very best friend in all the world but his friend didn't recognize him. From inside the stadium came a sound that started as a cheer but then choked and turned into a loud sigh.

''Nother Chitty!' gurgled Little Harry – reaching out for Chitty.

'No, it's the same Chitty, but younger,' said Lucy. 'You'd need to have some basic grasp of the theory of relativity to understand it properly. The point is, we are stranded in time. This car can travel in time. All we have to do is steal it.'

'Yes,' said Jem. 'Except if we stole it, that would be stealing, wouldn't it?'

'I suppose,' Lucy suggested with a shrug, 'we could ask the Pott family nicely for a lift back to our own time.'

'I suppose,' said Jem, reaching out to flick the propellers of the Lightning one last time. He was thinking – Yes, it would be wrong to steal this car, but to have to ask someone else for a ride in Chitty Chitty Bang Bang . . . That felt even wronger.

'I think,' said Lucy, 'that it's probably best to hand over this moral dilemma to our parents.'

Mum and Dad were staring at the newspaper seller's transistor radio, hypnotized by the match commentary.

'The word today,' Dad sighed, 'is *a game of two halves.*'

'Mum, Dad,' said Jem, 'we've found Chitty Chitty—'

'Shh,' shushed Mum. 'There're just three minutes left of the first half.'

'But, Mum—'

At that moment, there was the roar of an engine. Jem spun round. Lucy spun round. Even Mum and Dad managed to tear themselves away from the football for a moment, just in time to see a flash of brass and a flicker of silver as Chitty Chitty Bang Bang sped away from the stadium.

'No!' gasped Lucy. 'The Potts are leaving! Our one guaranteed ride out of this godforsaken era with its jingly bells and horrible jolly colours.'

'How could they leave before the end of the match?' said Dad. 'Why would anyone do that?'

'Come on! We've got to follow them,' pleaded Jem.

'The idea of following a twelve-cylinder, twenty-three-litre Paragon Panther on foot,' said Lucy, 'is poignant but pointless.'

'Here, mate, give my car a push, will you?' The speaker was a man in a smart blue uniform, peaked hat and shiny boots.

'Can't it wait until after the game?' said Mum.

'Sorry, madam.' The man shrugged. 'This here is a national emergency.'

He pointed towards a long black limousine with a little flag flying from its bonnet. In the back seat was a young woman fiddling impatiently with her unusually sparkly hat.

'Is that . . . ?' gasped Dad.

'. . . the Queen of England?' said Mum.

'And lots of other places,' added the chauffeur. 'There's been an occurrence at the Houses of Parliament. Got to get there at the double. But the blooming car won't start.'

'What seems to be the trouble?' said Dad.

Mum curtsied and Dad bowed as they passed the royal vehicle. The Queen gave them each a slightly mechanical wave.

'She waved at me,' breathed Mum. Then she called, in a voice that was loud but respectful, 'Don't you worry, Your Majesty, Mr Tooting will have this sorted out in a jiffy.'

'Open the bonnet,' said Dad, 'and give me two minutes.'

'Really?' said the chauffeur. 'Don't mind me saying, but this is an unusually complicated engine and you seem to have unusually fat fingers.'

Dad hated

anyone mentioning his fat fingers. He clenched his fists in fury, but Mum calmed things down. 'They may be fat,' she said, 'but they are attached to a mechanical genius.'

The chauffeur shrugged and unlatched the bonnet. 'I'm opening this,' he said, 'purely to demonstrate that there is no point in opening it. The engine is very old-fashioned.'

Dad stared at the powerful engine that now lay revealed in the sunlight. 'I'm used to old-fashioned engines,' he admitted. 'The word today is *teeny-tiny problem with the carburettor cooling flange* . . .' He tugged and twisted a few things. The car gave one last puff of smoke, then seemed to sigh contentedly as its carburettor cooled down. Then the engine roared.

'Remarkable,' said the chauffeur, shaking Dad's hand. 'I'm sure the Queen will give you a thank-you wave as we drive by.'

But the Queen didn't give a thank-you wave. She wound down the window and called, 'You there, Mr Tooting. Hop in.'

'Oh no, Dad, don't,' begged Jem. 'Think of Chitty . . .'

'Shhhh, Jem,' muttered Mum. 'You can't say no to the Queen.'

'Is this your family?' said the Queen. 'Do tell them to hop in too.'

Mum chivvied the children into the car, warning them to smile and say thank you and telling them this was the lift of a lifetime.

'Yes,' said Lucy, 'but this isn't our lifetime. We aren't going to be born for fifty years.'

'Do get in,' said the Queen. 'Plenty of room if you all squidge up. Ready, Soapy? Step on the gas. Soapy is the name of my chauffeur, by the way. And I'm . . .'

'The Queen of England,' said Mum a bit too quickly.

'. . . and Lots of Other Places,' added the Queen sniffily.

Dad introduced himself and the rest of the family.

'I'm most awfully grateful to you for fixing the car,' the Queen said. 'I don't know how to thank you.'

'Cash would be nice,' said Lucy.

'Lucy,' hissed Mum, 'you can't just ask the Queen for cash like that. Do it like this: Cash would be nice, Your Majesty.'

'The Queen doesn't carry cash,' said the Queen.

'Tell you what, I'll knight you soon as I have a moment. Got to sort out this dashed national emergency first of course. I'm sick as a parrot about missing the match. Did you see any of it?'

'We were listening on the radio.'

'I'm most fearfully anxious about it. Why has he picked Geoff Hurst? Surely Jimmy Greaves is the better striker. If we don't win, I'm going to pack this whole Queen thing in. I mean, really, what's the point in ruling a country that always loses?'

'Don't worry, Your Majesty,' soothed Mum. 'England will win, definitely.'

'Four–two after extra time,' specified Dad.

The Queen gave him a searching look. 'How on earth can you know that? Do you read the future as well as fixing engines? What a fascinating man your father is, children. I feel he is just the man to sort out this national emergency.'

Fast as a rocket and smooth as chocolate they sped down the A4088 to the North Circular and east towards the A5. Through traffic lights, over roundabouts, they slid through Swinging London. There were Union Jacks. Red buses. Black cabs. Policemen with dome-shaped hats riding round on bicycles.

'I love the Sixties!' said Mum.

'Yes, everything's so modern now, isn't it?' agreed the Queen. 'Look at this, for instance . . .' She twisted a knob on her armrest. A panel opened in her door and a gloved robot hand – beautifully dressed in silk and lace – popped out and began to wave to the empty streets. 'For centuries monarchs wore themselves out waving at people. Now that we're in the 1960s, I've got this to do all my royal waving for me. Saves frightful wear and tear on the royal elbow, and allows one to get on with one's knitting.'

'We've got some terrific gadgets in our car too,' said Dad. 'There's even a thing that pops wine gums into your mouth if you get stressed while you're driving.'

'You never mentioned that,' said Mum.

'I thought if other people knew about it, they might eat all the wine gums.'

'Soapy, switch on the radio,' said the Queen. 'We're missing the game.'

All the way down Regent Street the Queen's automatic Royal Wave Machine karate-chopped backwards and forwards so fast it was just a blur, while the Queen herself leaned forward, listening to every kick of the match.

'This is so exciting,' whispered Mum, snuggling up to Dad. 'You are now car mechanic by royal appointment. We really could live like this.'

When they stopped outside the Palace of Westminster the Queen peered out of the car.

'Well,' she said, 'everything looks normal enough, but what's that noise?'

The air was filled with a strange throbbing sound. Jem could see now that a huge crowd had gathered.

Dad got out of the car. The paving stones were vibrating slightly, as were the kerbstones. The water in the Thames was bubbling as though it was a giant jacuzzi. It was the unmistakable sound of something massive about to happen.

'I don't suppose you've had any warnings?' asked Dad. 'About earthquakes, for instance?'

'The epicentre,' said Lucy, 'appears to be Big Ben. The leaves on the trees here are shaking, but in front of the tower whole trees are rocking. Look.'

The throbbing noise grew louder. First it was worryingly loud, then it was frighteningly loud. People began to run across Westminster Bridge to the south side of the river.

'What is going on?' asked the Queen.

'It's not what's going on that's worrying me,' said Dad. 'It's what is about to go off.'

The moment he said this there was a huge explosion around the base of the tower of Big Ben. The whole tower shook. It looked as though it was going to come crashing down.

But it didn't come crashing down.

It did something much, much more surprising.

2

BBC NEWSFLASH: EXTRAORDINARY OCCURRENCE AT THE PALACE OF WESTMINSTER . . .

There are reports of an extraordinary occurrence at the Houses of Parliament. The BBC can confirm that at 15.55 today, while the rest of the world was watching the World Cup Final, the two-hundred-foot-tall tower of Big Ben – which has stood at the northern end of the Houses of Parliament for over a hundred years – flew away.

'There was a loud bang, and a lot of smoke,' said a London bobby, 'and then it took off like a rocket.' Londoners – including Her Majesty the Queen – watched in astonishment as the famous tower flew over north London, at a height of about four hundred feet. 'I could still see the time on the clock,' said one soldier who was on duty at Horse Guards Parade at the time.

'Whoever did this,' said the Queen, as Big Ben soared over the Embankment, 'is extremely irresponsible. What if it flies over Wembley and distracts our players? It could lose us the World Cup.'

'What if it lands on Washington or Moscow?' said Lucy. 'It could start a world war.'

'If it lands on Wembley itself,' said the Queen, 'it could lead to disqualification! Who would do a thing like this? Who would steal a two-hundred-foot-tall Gothic tower?'

A name was already beginning to hover on the edge of Jem's mind.

'Who would *want* to steal it?' said Mum.

The name in Jem's mind was 'Tiny Jack – supervillain'. Tiny Jack had already stolen the Sphinx and Stonehenge; of course he would want Big Ben.

A huge crowd was rolling up the Embankment to see the empty space where once the famous tower had stood. They were so horrified and amazed that barely any of them noticed the Queen sitting there in her car.

'This is a national disgrace,' said Her Majesty, shaking her head so that the diamonds on her crown sparkled like tears.

'Cheer up,' said Dad. 'After all, it's just a big clock. Whereas it's almost full time at Wembley, with both teams level at two–two. The word today is *extra time during which England score two more goals and win the World Cup.'*

'And Germany have scored!' barked the commentator, ***'with only seconds to go, it's three-two to Germany. Can England equalize? There really are only seconds on the clock. Some people are leaving. They think it's all over . . .'*** ***There was the piercing sound of a referee's whistle. '. . . It is now. Germany have beaten England and won the World Cup!'***

Mum stared at the radio in astonishment and despair. 'But,' she squeaked, 'we should've won!'

'Oh yes, we should've won,' growled the Queen. 'Of course we SHOULD have won. Where does SHOULD get you. Big Ben SHOULD be over there. But is it?'

'Typical England,' moaned Dad. 'The one time in history we win the cup, we go and lose it.'

'England were all over Germany for the first half,' blared the radio, ***'but the players seemed to get distracted when the tower of Big Ben flew over the stadium. The famous bell struck four and Germany struck out for goal. And now . . . I'm sorry, I can't say it . . . it's too sad.'***

'What a day!' sighed the Queen. 'The World Cup and the world's most famous clock tower, both lost in a single afternoon. It's treason, that's what this is. I'm still allowed to chop people's heads off for treason, so whoever did it had better watch out.'

'Talking of things going missing,' said Lucy, 'has anyone seen Little Harry?'

'Little Harry?' Mum looked around frantically. 'I thought he was with you?'

'Where did you last see him?' said Dad.

'When we were looking at Chitty Chitty Bang Bang,' said Jem. 'He was pretending to drive her.'

'Ga gooo ga!'

Lucy heard it first. She stuck her head out of the window and looked up and down the Embankment.

'Lucy, kindly behave in a more ladylike manner – there's a monarch present,' snapped Dad.

'Ga gooo ga!'

This time they all heard it. Then they all saw it – the plume of exhaust smoke billowing like a ribbon along the Embankment, the musical roar of a mighty engine, the flash of racing green. Chitty Chitty Bang Bang was just passing by.

'Little Harry!' gasped Mum. 'Stop that car!

'If a car needs to be stopped, I shall say so. After all I am the Queen,' said the Queen.

'But,' cried Jem, 'that was them!'

'Who?'

'The traitors who launched Big Ben!'

The Queen blinked. 'Soapy,' she commanded. 'Put your foot down. Follow that car! The rest of you, fasten your safety belts. Get ready for the queen of car chases!'

The brakes of the royal limousine squealed, its tyres coughed blue smoke, as Soapy swung the car around. The Tootings and the Queen were thrown from one side to the other as it charged on to the Embankment. A big red London bus was coming the other way. It squealed to a halt just in time. The driver pounded on its horn in fury. Though when the Queen glared at him through the window, he took off his cap and bowed his head.

Lucy gave Jem a hard look.

'We have to get Little Harry back.' He shrugged. 'We can explain the rest when we catch up.'

'Unless of course she chops off Commander Pott's head before you get the chance,' commented Lucy.

They could see Chitty Chitty Bang Bang ahead of them now. They were so close they could read GEN II on her number plate. Soapy flashed the royal headlights and tooted the royal horn (a melodious but slightly aggressive fanfare), to tell Chitty to stop in the name of the Queen. But Chitty did not stop. Instead she blew a great cloud of exhaust smoke into the royal limousine's path, then sped off faster than ever.

'Oh, that makes me mad,' said the Queen. 'What is the point of being a monarch if you can't stop traffic? Soapy, slow down – I want to talk to this London bobby.'

Just in front of Cleopatra's Needle was a young policeman on traffic duty. The Queen called him over. 'Bobby,' she said. 'Get on to Scotland Yard. Tell them to raise Tower Bridge. Quick about it.'

Before he had time to say 'Right away, Your Majesty' she was gone. At the Tower of London Chitty swerved to the right, powering on to the bridge.

'Now we've got them!' giggled the Queen. The two sections of road that make up Tower Bridge were slowly rising into the air. Already there was a wide, windy gap where the two used to touch.

But Chitty Chitty Bang Bang did not behave as expected. Her engines revved and banged. Her tyres spun. Her motor roared. Instead of rolling gently backwards, she ploughed right up the almost vertical road and shot into the air. The whole world seemed to hold its breath. Then there was a thud as she landed gently on the far side of the bridge and sped off south along the A100.

'We've lost her,' sighed Jem.

'I'm a monarch. Surely my car is more powerful than theirs? It's the law,' snarled the Queen. 'Rev it, Soapy.'

Soapy revved the engines. The mighty limousine roared up the still-rising bridge and shot into the air. 'God save the Queen!' whooped the Queen as they whistled over the Thames before landing on the other half of the bridge, which was now as steep as a slide. It slithered, skidded, slipped and finally smashed into a pillar box. There was no sign of Chitty.

'They've gone,' said Mum.

'Maybe we could head them off,' said Jem. 'I mean, they're probably heading back to their house, just off the A20(M) near Dover.'

'How on earth do you know where they live?' asked Dad.

'Their address was written inside the front page of the logbook. For some reason it stuck in my head.'

'Soapy!' commanded the Queen. 'Take us to Dover.'

'Certainly, ma'am, only . . .'

'At the double!'

'Yes, ma'am, but if I might just ask . . .' He turned his searchlight eyes on Jem. 'How does this little fella know so much about these Big Ben thieves?'

'Yes,' said the Queen. 'How *do* you know so much about them?' Her eyes narrowed. She stared at Jem. Jem squirmed. The Queen had been so helpful that it seemed wrong to lie to her, but the truth would take hours. The truth involved time travel, lost cities, piranhas, evil geniuses. Would she even believe it if he told her?

'Jem,' said Mum, 'it's always best to tell the truth.'

'And the truth is,' cut in Lucy, 'that Jem used to be a getaway driver – one of the best there's ever been. He knew all the worst criminals . . .'

'Really?' said the Queen. 'He looks so young.'

'A fact he used to his advantage,' said Lucy.

Jem gave Lucy a hard look.

'He's reformed now. He wants to make amends by fighting crime. Will you help him?'

'Soapy!' said the Queen. 'Get moving! The game's afoot!'

Soapy revved the engine.

'Luckily,' said the Queen, 'there there is a royal shortcut to Dover for use in times of national emergency. Please don't mention it to anyone as it's a secret.'

Halfway along Tower Bridge Road, Soapy steered left into a . . .

THE DESCRIPTION OF THIS PART OF THE JOURNEY HAS BEEN REMOVED FOR REASONS OF NATIONAL SECURITY.

. . . until they found themselves bowling along the open road with Chitty Chitty Bang Bang just a hundred metres or so ahead of them.

'Nearly caught him!' whooped the Queen.

Jem looked around. There was something strangely familiar about this stretch of road. Where were they? There were no road signs. Or rather there was one but it had been knocked over and was now face down in the hedge.

'Mum! Dad! Soapy! Your Majesty! I know where this is! Slow down!'

'What?'

'We're coming up to Bucklewing Corner – the slipperiest and most unpredictable bend in the road in the world. Please . . .'

'Certainly,' said Soapy. 'I hate dangerous bends.'

Gently the royal limousine slowed its pace. Cautiously it advanced along the road. Up ahead of them, Chitty Chitty Bang Bang did none of those things. She went faster and faster. Just beyond her they could see a line of trees. That must be where the road bent back, thought Jem. Then he stopped thinking all together. There was a flash of light.

There was a sound like a massive bowling ball running through a forest of small trees. There was a ball of smoke and a flash of fire.

'Look!' shouted Jem.

'I can't look,' sobbed Soapy. 'It's too tragic.' Respectfully he took off his chauffeur's cap and covered his face.

'Don't do that while you're driving!' snapped Her Majesty, as the royal limousine zigzagged out of control. Mum reached over the seat and grabbed the wheel. In all the fuss and panic, only Jem noticed something strange and startling. Out of the ball of smoke and flames where Chitty had crashed through the hedge had shot two plumes of smoke, powering up into the bright blue sky like firework rockets. But unlike rockets they didn't explode into clouds of glitter; instead they seemed to come close together and stop in mid-air, almost as if they were looking down on the wreck, almost as if they were talking to each other.

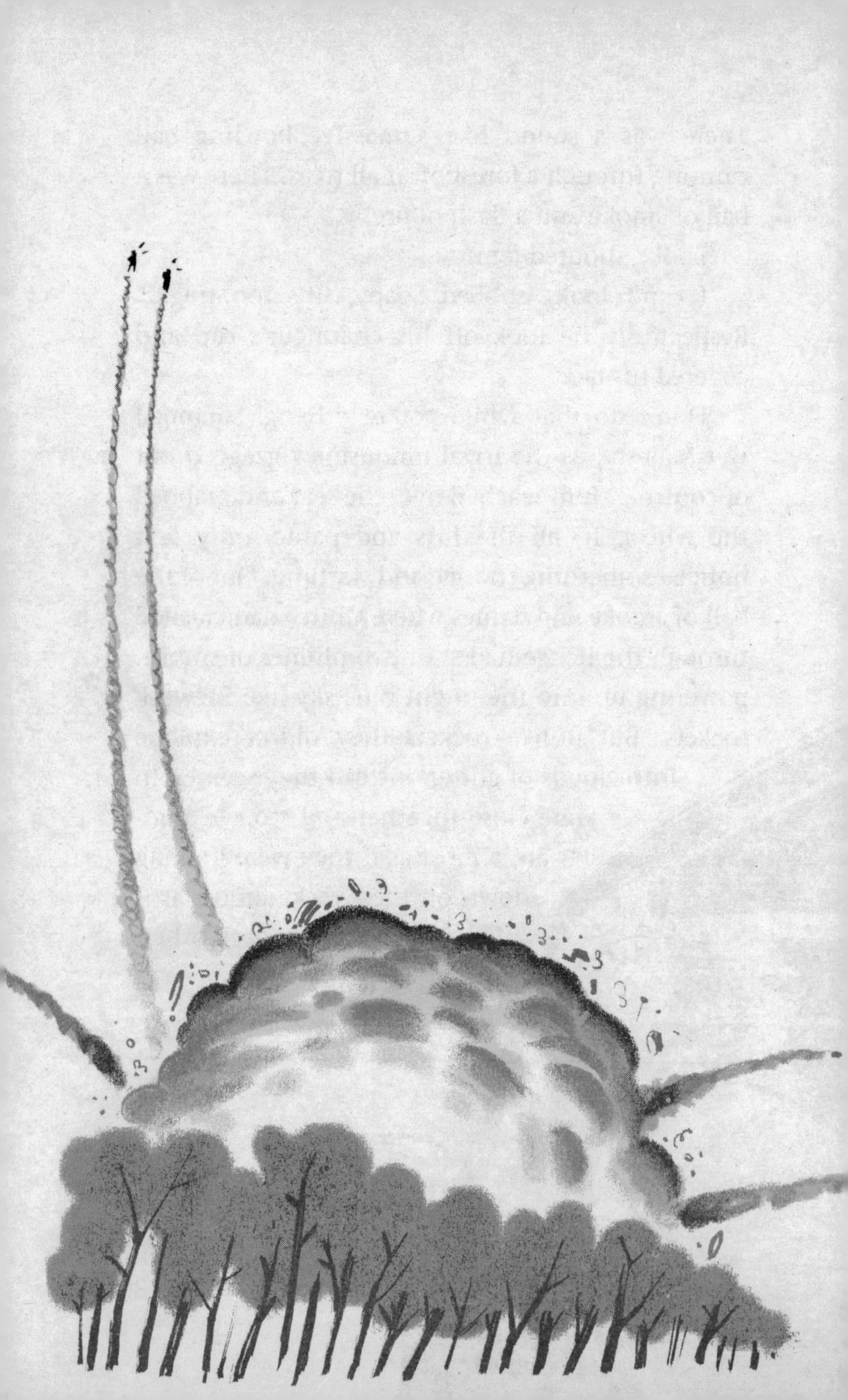

3

The notorious bend at Bucklewing Corner was first mentioned as an accident black spot back in the Domesday Book in 1086. King John lost part of his Crown Jewels here when he was running away from the French too fast in 1216. He failed to slow down in time and his treasure coach crashed into the field. Over hundreds of years, hundreds of carts, coaches and cars had also crashed here. Now the field beyond the corner looked like the scene of a motor massacre. And there among the broken-down saloons and wrecked racers, lay the smouldering remains of the most beautiful car ever built – Chitty Chitty Bang Bang.

'Little Harry,' sobbed Mum. 'Little Harry!' she called.

'Soapy, go and look for survivors,' said the Queen.

They all searched the wreckage, but there was no sign of life.

A young man in a sharp blue suit with a narrow black tie and shiny, shiny hair strode up to them across the field of broken cars, waving a clipboard. 'All vehicles that overshoot the bend,' he said, 'revert to the ownership of Bucklewing Scrap and Salvage.' He clicked his biro impatiently. 'Sign here, please.' It was as he was handing her the forms to sign that he recognized the Queen. 'Your Majesty,' he stuttered, dropping on one knee. 'You're very welcome here. As was your illustrious ancestor King John in 1216. I'm Hornblower Bucklewing the Eleventh.'

'I don't suppose you've seen any treacherous types hereabouts?' asked the Queen. 'Someone has stolen Big Ben.'

'It was on the radio, ma'am,' said Bucklewing. 'London is in a state of panic. First the defeat in the World Cup, then Big Ben was stolen and now they say that you are lost without trace.'

'I'm not lost,' said the Queen. 'I'm just in Kent.'

'In London all anyone knows is that you vanished during half-time.'

A thoughtful look spread over the Queen's face. 'If they think we've vanished, Soapy,' she said, 'couldn't we sort of . . . stay vanished? Couldn't we take the car and . . . disappear. Couldn't we just ride away to Paris, or Egypt, or look for lost cities or the North Pole. I've always wanted to see the North Pole.'

'Me too,' said Dad.

'Majesty,' said Soapy, 'London is in a state of panic. Your people are frightened and sad. One wave from you and all would be well. As one of your subjects, I can tell you that when I'm feeling blue nothing cheers me like the smile on your cheeky royal face.'

'Oh all right, don't go on about it,' she muttered, trudging off towards her car.

'I'll see you to your motor car, ma'am.'

'If you find those traitors,' called the Queen over her shoulder as she waved goodbye, 'I'll ennoble you all or something.'

The Tootings looked despondently at the wreck of Chitty Chitty Bang Bang.

'Where can Little Harry be?' sobbed Mum.

'Perhaps he wasn't in Chitty after all,' said Dad, considering the damage to the car. 'You know, she looks bad, but I really think she can be fixed.'

Jem glanced upward. The two plumes of smoke he had noticed earlier were no longer climbing into the sky. In fact, they were plummeting down towards them like guided missiles. Closer and closer they came. As they swooped closer, Jem could see that they seemed to have faces. Stern, staring faces wearing big black goggles. They whistled over the Tootings' heads, close enough to ruffle their hair. They dropped down on the grass. They were children! A blonde little girl and a dark-haired boy, each wearing a pair of flying goggles and a jet pack. The girl peered at the Tootings through her goggles. The huge lenses made her look like a big, furious insect.

'Who are you?' said Mum.

'I know who they are,' said Jem. 'You're Jemima and Jeremy Pott, aren't you?'

'Yes, we are.' The girl smiled. 'Was that the Queen just now? Are you friends of hers?'

'No. She just gave us a lift.'

'Jeremy and Jemima Pott!' said Dad. 'This is a very exciting moment for us. We're big fans of your father's work. I mean . . . Chitty Chitty Bang Bang – what a car. I'm a mechanic myself, you know, so I appreciate the finer points of—'

'We're looking,' interrupted Mum, 'for our little son. He was last seen sitting in your car – in Chitty Chitty Bang Bang – pretending to drive it.'

'Yes, he was there when we drove off,' said Jemima. 'We felt sorry for him. I wanted to adopt him. He was sweet – he kept wanting to use our jet packs.'

'Wow,' said Dad. 'Jet packs. I always wanted a jet pack. Did your father invent them?'

'Yes,' said Jeremy.

'What a genius.'

'Never mind about jet packs,' snapped Mum. 'Where is Little Harry?'

'Oh. That was all a bit strange,' explained the girl. 'We were watching the World Cup Final. Father had the Remote Control Big Ben launcher in his pocket. He was going to press the button the moment the final whistle went. Suddenly the countdown counter started to turn. Someone had initiated the launch sequence. Naturally we all jumped into Chitty Chitty Bang Bang and set off to try to stop it. When we got there, Big Ben was—'

'Don't say any more,' interrupted Jeremy. 'This is all top secret. Even the Queen didn't know about it.'

'Your father turned Big Ben into a rocket?' said Dad. 'What a genius!'

'Yes, he is a genius,' said Jeremy.

'It was supposed to be a lovely surprise,' said Jemima. 'Big Ben was going to fly all around the world ringing its chimes to celebrate England winning the World Cup. Now it's all spoilt.'

'Get to Little Harry,' said Mum.

'Big Ben was making a terrible racket. Little Harry – so funny – he came with us to see what was wrong. Mimsie and Daddy dashed inside to try to save the nation and told us to wait in the car. While we were waiting a lady dressed all in red, with red hair, came over and looked at Chitty . . .'

'Oh no!' Mum gasped. 'I know what's coming next. Don't say any more. Oh. Yes. Do – tell us everything.'

'We weren't surprised she was looking at Chitty.

People are always looking at her because she is so beautiful. But then Chitty gave a blast on her Klaxon. She does that when she's upset.'

'I gave the lady a hard stare,' said Jeremy.

'Which was brave of you because she did look quite fierce. But she seemed to know Little Harry. She said his name. "Hello, Little Harry," she said. "How would you like to come and play a game?"'

'Little Harry knows better than to talk to strangers,' said Mum.

'She didn't seem like a stranger. It seemed like he remembered her from somewhere.'

Little Harry did indeed remember seeing the lady dressed in red before. He was just a bit hazy about some of the details. He remembered her being nice and smiley and something about food. Somehow he did not remember that the food in question was himself and that she had been going to feed him to a pool of piranhas.

'The lady said her motto was "Fun, fun, fun". And Little Harry said "FUN!" really loudly, just like that. Then she asked him what his favourite kind of fun was.'

'Dinosaurs,' said Mum, through her tears.

'That's exactly what he said – dinosaurs. And do you know what the woman did then? She opened her handbag and took out a dinosaur egg of the kind a stegosaurus might lay. Isn't that extraordinary – what kind of woman would just happen to have a dinosaur egg in her purse? The little chap seemed terribly excited about it. He trotted after her into Big Ben with a smile on his face. Oh dear, should we have stopped him?'

Mum was too upset to reply.

'Anyway, the next thing we knew, there was a deafening explosion and a blinding flash and Big Ben took off with Mimsie and Daddy and the woman in red . . .'

'. . . and Little Harry . . .'

'. . . all on board. Goodness knows what's going to happen to them.' As Jemima said this she looked up at the sky, trying to imagine the fate that awaited them all.

'The woman in red,' explained Jem, 'is called the Nanny. She looks after a very small evil genius called Tiny Jack. We believe it was Tiny Jack who detonated the Big Ben rocket with your parents on board.'

'And now she's got Little Harry.' Mum grasped Dad's hand in despair.

'I'm sure my father will deal with this Jack fellow in no time,' Jeremy said with confidence. 'Especially if he's tiny. Father is six foot two. He used to be in the Navy. He's also a genius.'

'It's not as simple as that,' said Jem. 'Tiny Jack is a thief. He'll steal anything – the Sphinx, Stonehenge, the Pyramids. But most of all he likes to steal cars. In fifty years' time he will steal this car –' he pointed to the wreckage of Chitty Chitty Bang Bang – 'and use her as the greatest getaway car ever. He could use her to steal all the gold from ancient El Dorado and escape into the future . . .'

'But that would change the course of history,' objected Jemima. 'Father said we must never travel in time unless we are accompanied by a responsible adult.'

'Tiny Jack would probably think that was fun,' said Lucy.

'*Fun?!*' exclaimed Jeremy. 'To make England lose the World Cup?'

'His idea of fun,' explained Lucy, 'is different from ours. He plays snakes and ladders with real snakes . . . What's the time, Mr Wolf? with an actual wolf. He wants to be the greatest supervillain the world has ever known.'

'But we can stop him,' said Jem, 'with the help of you and Chitty Chitty Bang Bang.'

Jeremy pointed out that Chitty Chitty Bang Bang was now a smouldering wreck.

'The word today,' said Dad, 'is *patch and mend*. We're in probably the greatest scrapyard in the world. This scrapyard is a compendium of British engineering genius. I'm sure I can get Chitty Chitty Bang Bang up and running in no time. The word today is *joining forces to defeat evil supervillains.*'

'We can do it,' said Jem, 'as long as we have Chitty Chitty Bang Bang.' He almost added that this was what Chitty wanted, this was why she had brought them to 1966. But he didn't say that, for fear that they would think he was mad.

'Chitty will save them,' said Jemima, as if she could hear Jem's thoughts. 'When we were kidnapped by gangsters, she took Mummy and Daddy right to their hiding place. I think she really cares about us.'

'Yes,' said Jem, a bit too enthusiastically. But that was all right. No one heard him anyway because . . .

'Ga gooo ga!!!!'

Everyone swung round to look at Chitty. While they had been talking, Hornblower Bucklewing XI had attached a length of chain to her radiator and now that chain was taut and quivering. Whatever was on the other end of the chain was pulling the car towards itself with incredible strength.

'Oh, good,' said Jeremy. 'Bucklewing's got her the right way up again.'

But Chitty did not agree. Her mighty wheels ran backwards, her engine screamed, as she pulled with all her mechanical muscle against the chain.

'Look!' said Lucy, pointing down the long avenue of smashed saloon cars and abandoned tyres towards a machine – a towering metal machine, shaped like a huge mouth. Its tongue was a long black conveyor belt. For teeth it had two rows of jagged metal spikes. For a stomach it had a thumping great crusher that pumped slowly up and down like a slow-motion fist. A rusty old pickup truck wobbled up the conveyor belt and into the machine's mouth. Glass splintered. Steel twisted. Tyres exploded. Rubber burned blue. Then out of the other end came a perfect metal cube, about the size of an old television set.

Chitty was the next in the queue.

'He's feeding Chitty into a car crusher!' gasped Mum.

'I'll stop him!' called Dad, sprinting off towards the machine, yelling, 'Mr Bucklewing! Mr Bucklewing!'

'He'll never make it!' wailed Jemima.

She's right, thought Jem. He hurled himself after Chitty. He vaulted over her door. He jumped into her front seat. He stamped on her brakes. Still the chain dragged her towards the jaws. He pulled on the handbrake. Her wheels locked tight. But still the machine pulled, sledging Chitty through the

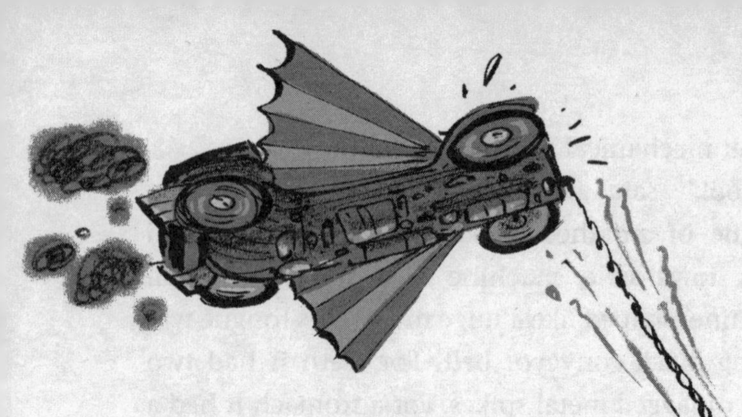

splurging mud. Wings, thought Jem. 'Surely she can fly out of here . . .' He pulled on the flight lever. Chitty's chassis shuddered as she engaged her wings. A yellow light flashed the message

in thick black letters on top of the flight lever, adding the word

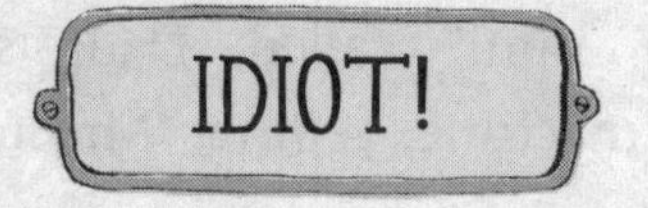

in even thicker letters. Even though he was possibly about to be crushed to death, Jem allowed himself a smile. Chitty had never communicated with him in actual words before. He pressed the accelerator. He shifted gear. Instead of trying to back away from the terrible machine, Chitty raced towards it. There was a familiar jolt, the jolt that always came when her wings caught the wind. The rushing air pinned Jem right back in his seat. 'Whoopeee!' he yelled, as Chitty soared into the air and skimmed over the top of the crushing machine. Chitty twisted in the air triumphantly.

The triumph lasted exactly forty-two seconds.

Having twisted once, Chitty Chitty Bang Bang twisted again. And again. Until Jem was sick and dizzy. Looking down, he saw his family waving at him wildly. He couldn't hear what they were shouting over the hungry mechanical chomping of the crusher. But it was obvious what they were trying to say. Chitty might be in the air, but the chain was still attached to her radiator. Link by link the chain was hauling her back towards those massive jaws.

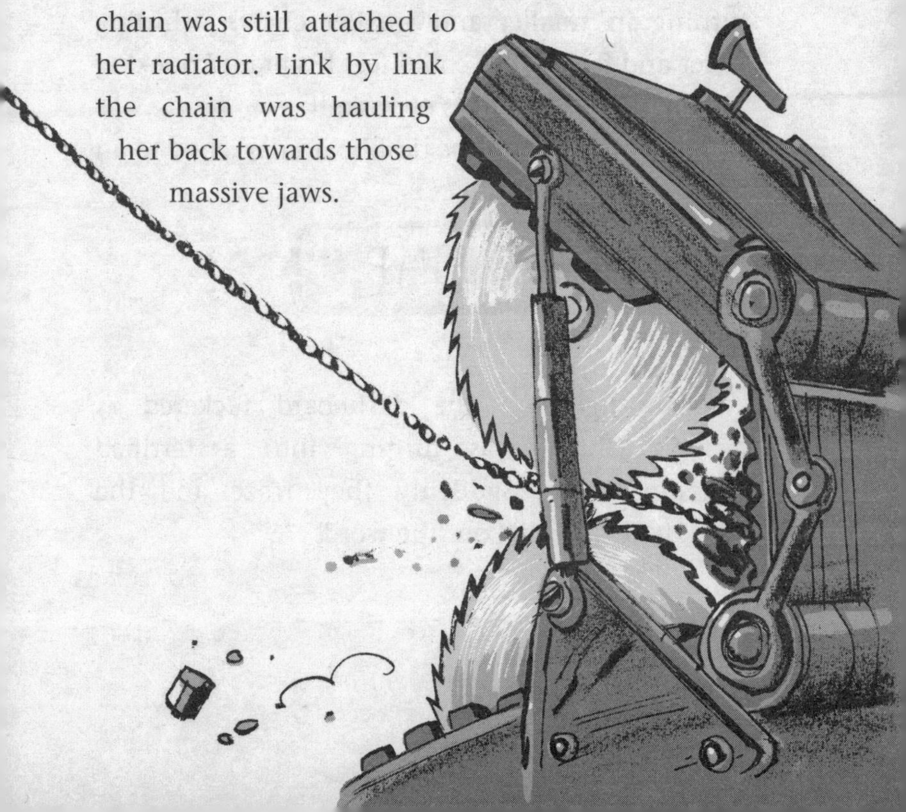

Jem searched the dashboard. There were buttons that adjusted the wing mirrors, the mudguards, the angle of the seats, but there seemed to be nothing that could save him. 'Come on, Chitty,' he breathed, 'give me a clue.'

A light on the dashboard glowed pink. Black letters appeared across it.

'No!' snarled Jem. There must be something he could do. Could he crawl along the bonnet and unhook the chain? By now Chitty was turning and turning in smaller and smaller circles, whirling faster and faster. Jem could feel his brain knocking against the inside of his own skull.

The pink light on the dashboard darkened to an angry red.

'Never!'

Every light on the dashboard flickered as though Chitty was turning into a terrified Christmas tree. Suddenly they froze and the black letters spelled out the words across them all.

Before he had time to wonder what this meant, Jem felt his ears being pressed against the sides of his head . . .

his head being pushed down into his neck . . .

his knees being forced up into his stomach . . .

and his stomach turning somersaults.

The trees turned somersaults too . . .

and so did the clouds.

Clouds and trees appeared and disappeared in sequence as though the whole world was in a washing machine.

Then . . . thud. He was sitting on top of a broken bus. But somehow he was still in the lovely leather driver's chair, staring straight ahead, trying to figure out why the view had changed. Whereas before he was looking at spinning trees, now all he could see was a massive noisy machine gnashing its way towards the back end of the car that was hanging out of its jaws. The registration of the car was GEN II so that car must be . . . wait! No!

It couldn't be!

Chitty had activated her ejector seat and sent Jem rocketing to safety.

'Ga gooo . . .'

. . . Nothing.

There was a terrible crunch. It sounded like a massive cube of metal falling from the top of a huge metal machine, on to a pile of scrap metal. It was made by a massive cube of metal falling from the top of a huge metal machine, on to a pile of scrap metal. That cube of metal had once been Chitty Chitty Bang Bang.

4

Everyone stared at the Cube of Metal That Had Once Been Chitty Chitty Bang Bang. No one knew what to say.

Hornblower Bucklewing XI strode over, carrying a big basket. 'I saved the picnic for you.' He smiled over the top of the creaking hamper. 'It was strapped to the back bumper. Lots of goodies in here.'

Slowly Jeremy looked up at him. 'You squashed our car,' he said.

'Legally it was my car. Once anything comes through that hedge, it belongs to the Bucklewing Scrap and Salvage Company. Always has done right back to the Royal Charter of 1216.'

'You squashed the most beautiful car on Earth,' snarled Jemima.

'Oh, come on. It was really old-fashioned.'

Bucklewing shrugged. 'This is 1966. We want things to be modern and speedy. Your car was really old-fashioned and square.'

'Chitty Chitty Bang Bang is not square,' said Jemima with a sniff.

'Not any more.' Hornblower smiled. 'Now she's a cube.' He put the picnic hamper down on top of the cube. 'Look it's sort of a trendy table now. I'm going to crush all these old-fashioned cars. They've been here so long, just getting old and rusty. That's why I bought this brand-new, ultra-modern car crusher. I'm going to clean this place up and make it look modern and with-it.'

'She doesn't look like a table,' said Lucy. 'She looks like a gravestone – the gravestone of the most fabulous car in history.'

Jem looked at the Cube of Metal That Had Once Been Chitty Chitty Bang Bang. He thought of all the terrible things that were happening simply because that car was no longer a car – his own little brother was stuck in a rocket-propelled Big Ben heading for a crash landing who knew where.

So were Commander and Mimsie Pott, and with them all hope of defeating Tiny Jack. The whole world could be destroyed, all because of this cube of metal.

No one knew what to say, but Dad had a go.

'Children,' he said, 'you must be feeling sad and frightened. After all, your parents could be about to sink into the Pacific, or smash into a Himalaya, or plop into a volcano. I'd just like to say that the Tooting family is at your service. If there's anything we can do to help . . .'

'That's very kind of you,' said Jeremy, 'but I'm sure we'll manage. Thanks anyway. Shame we can't save the world together.' He attached wires to the corners of the Cube of Metal That Had Once Been Chitty Chitty Bang Bang. The wires were attached to the twins' tool belts. They had strapped on their jet packs and were preparing to fly away.

'Goodbye,' said Jemima, shaking Dad's hand. 'I do apologize if Jeremy offended you with his remarks about your fingers. You're welcome to the picnic.'

'Thanks,' said Dad, taking the picnic basket and looking inside.

'But you can't just go,' pleaded Jem.

'Good afternoon,' said Jeremy. 'Enjoy the picnic.'

'No, wait! There must be something we can do. Your father is a top-secret inventor. Maybe one of his top-secret inventions . . .'

'Father's top-secret inventions,' said Jeremy, 'are top secret.'

The twins pulled down their goggles. There was a blast of smoke, a flash of flame and, whoosh, they were gone, hauling the last sad remains of Chitty Chitty Bang Bang dangling in the air behind them.

5

For a long time, the Tootings just watched the Pott twins and the Cube of Metal That Had Once Been Chitty Chitty Bang Bang soaring over the woods and into the twilight. A chill crept into the air. Night came.

'At least we've still got this terrific picnic,' said Dad, lifting the lid of the handsome hamper to reveal a row of bottles of homemade lemonade, some cold sausages, a pot of mustard, strawberry puffs and a bag of boiled sweets.

'How can you think of food at a time like this?' wailed Mum. 'Little Harry is lost.'

'You're right,' said Dad, closing the lid solemnly. 'I'll just have one of these.' He put one of the sweets in his mouth. It was in fact one of Commander Pott's inventions: Crackpot's

Whistling Sweets – you suck and they whistle.

'If only we'd never found Chitty Chitty Bang Bang,' sighed Mum.

'Tweet tweet,' went Dad.

'None of this would have happened.'

'Toot toot.'

'If only we had carried on living our nice little life in our nice little . . . would you please stop whistling?'

But we didn't find Chitty, thought Jem. She found us really. Dad didn't really restore her, she restored herself. Whenever they went on their adventures, who decided on the destination? No matter how carefully they planned, how many maps and sandwiches they took, they always seemed to end up somewhere unexpected. Unexpected to them. But not to Chitty.

But if Chitty was in charge, then why were they here now? Why would she let Little Harry be kidnapped? Why would she allow Commander Pott – the man who created her – to be shot into the sky in a brick rocket?

As his thoughts wandered, so did Jem. He tramped through the grass and branches, without looking where he was going. Suddenly he noticed that his feet were wet. He looked up to see a little lake. Moonlight was already silvering its water.

Something was rippling that moonlight. A rowing boat was sliding quietly towards him.

'Jem!' hissed a girl's voice. 'Jem, come on. Get in.'

'Jemima?'

'Shhh. Come on.'

Mud squished into Jem's shoes as he squelched through the shallows and clambered into the boat.

'I've muffled the oars, so no one will hear us.' She lifted the oars out of the water. The blades were wrapped in thick beach towels. 'What do you think? Clever, eh?'

'Yes. Really clever.'

'For a girl.'

'For anyone. Where are we going?'

Jemima shook her head and put a finger to her lips. They rowed in silence. Every now and then the water would gulp as a fish swam away from them. Some frogs plopped into the water from the log on which they were resting. An owl shrieked. Skilful and silent, Jemima steered the boat to the far side of the lake. It sliced into the mossy bank. She stepped out and held the boat steady while Jem clambered after her. There was a small jetty, but they didn't tie the boat to it. Instead, they dragged it in among the trees where no one could see it.

Once they were hidden in the shadows, Jemima

whispered, 'I thought it was very brave, the way you tried to save Chitty Chitty Bang Bang.'

'Er . . . oh,' muttered Jem. 'Thanks.'

'Jeremy is brave too,' she whispered. 'He would have done the same as you, if he'd thought of it. I'm sorry he was so hard on you. He was sad about Chitty being destroyed. And about our parents being kidnapped. I think he was worried that

he was going to blub. Daddy doesn't approve of blubbing in front of people.'

'Wow,' said Jem. For there in front of them was a lovely white farmhouse, and next to it a big barn of a building with a glass dome on top and huge wooden doors.

'Father's secret workshop. It used to be some kind of boathouse. He changed it round himself. That's his observatory up there in the roof.' She pulled a metal handle and the doors swung open on well-oiled hinges. 'This is where he does all his secret inventing. I thought if you had a look inside, you might be able to think of something we can do to save them. I'm sure Jeremy would love you to help, but he thinks it's a bit wet to ask. It's all right for me to ask of course because I'm just a girl.'

Jem stepped inside. Moonlight filtered through the slats in the woodwork and silvered the rows of bottles and racks of tools. 'Where's the light switch?'

'I'm not sure. I've brought a torch.' The powerful beam split the gloom. The first thing it hit was a grinning skull looking down at her. She screamed.

'It's all right,' whispered Jem. 'It's just a skeleton. Look, it's hanging from a stand. We've got one in school, in the biology lab.'

'I know,' said Jemima, 'but a scream is the proper ladylike response to a skeleton in the dark, don't you think?' Huge shadows danced across the walls as she swept the whole barn with her torch. 'I've never been in here before. Father and Jeremy do all the inventing. Mother and I make the sandwiches.'

'I see.'

'Oh look! I remember when he invented these . . .' On the shelf was a row of what looked like square potatoes.

'What are they?'

'Square potatoes,' said Jemima. 'Father thought they'd be so much easier to chop and peel. He thought they would revolutionize the great British chip shop.'

'Didn't they?'

'Each individual potato had to be grown inside its own metal box. It was quite an expensive way to grow potatoes. Also sometimes the box wouldn't undo properly. The square potatoes were easier to chop but a lot, lot harder to grow.' Her torch wandered over test tubes, blackboards, a huge cooker, bits of engine, piles of wheels. 'This is so exciting!' she said. 'Oh look!' She held up something that looked like a green frisbee with a hole in the middle. 'Now this is really fab.'

'What is it?'

'Edible gramophone records.'

'Edible what?'

'Gramophone records. You know, with music on them.' She placed the green disc carefully on a kind of turntable, and flicked a switch. The disc spun round and round and music came out. Jemima swayed and swung to the music and joined in the chorus: 'What's new pussycat?'

'Come on,' she teased. 'Don't be so square.'

'I was thinking about your mum and dad,' said Jem.

'Oh! I forgot! I'm so easily distracted, being a girl. Oh dear! Just think – if we can't save them, Jeremy and I will be orphans.'

Jem finally spotted the light switch. With the lights on he could see that the 'lab' was crazily cluttered. Piles of motor components lay on a big desk next to a collection of birds' eggs and snake skins. A huge stuffed grizzly bear was peering at a blackboard covered in complicated formulae and diagrams, as though it was trying to crack a difficult equation.

'Cecile!' Jemima gasped. Cecile was the grizzly bear apparently. 'She looks so sad without her brother. Her brother was Charles Henry, but Daddy used him as the test pilot for his antigravity paint.'

'Antigravity paint? Did it work?'

'Of course it worked. All Daddy's inventions work. How can you even ask?'

'It's just that I'm from the future, and in the future we don't have antigravity paint, so clearly it didn't catch on. You would think that if something as useful as antigravity paint had been invented, people would be using it all the time.'

'I suppose it might have been a bit *too* antigravity,' admitted Jemima. She glanced up at the roof. There was a big, splintery hole in the ceiling next to the glass dome – just about the size of hole that a stuffed grizzly bear might make if it smashed through the ceiling.

'I see,' said Jem.

'And after all, it's working for Big Ben.'

'Big Ben is flying on *antigravity paint*?'

'Daddy used rocket engines to get it off the ground, but it's staying up there through a combination of antigravity paint and the centripetal force exerted by the Earth. He has so many brilliant ideas. Look at this for instance . . .' She pointed to one of those shopping bags on wheels that you pull behind you. It had a small satellite dish poking out of the top. 'That is a phone that you can take on journeys. A mobile phone. Imagine that. Daddy and Mimsie are always trying to think up ways to make the world into a better place. With fewer wars and less traffic and more talking and fun.'

'Hello? Hello, Jemima?'

Jemima's eyes widened. 'Listen,' she cried. 'That's Daddy's voice! Where is he?'

'Jemima? Jeremy? Can you hear us?'

'And that's Mummy! Mummy, where are you?'

'Jemima? Jeremy?'

Jemima followed the voice, pushing over towers

of boxes, scrabbling across cluttered work benches, clambering into the darkest corner of the lab.

'Mummy! Daddy! Where are you? How did you get here? Oh.'

Crouching on the floor, behind a spaghetti of wires and valves, was Jeremy, speaking into a fat microphone that looked like an electric tennis racket. It was connected to a radio the size of a caravan. 'Kent calling Big Ben,' he said, without looking up. 'Kent calling Big Ben. Do you read me?'

'Big Ben to Kent. Big Ben to Kent. Reading you loud and clear, Kent.' The voice of Commander Caractacus Pott came crackling through the radio.

'Thank goodness you're alive,' said Jeremy.

'Of course we're alive! First things first – how did England do at Wembley?'

'I'm afraid we lost three–two. We were distracted by Big Ben flying over.'

'Oh blow. Never mind. We're approaching the White Cliffs of Dover at a height of about twenty thousand feet. It's taken us just one hundred and eighty-eight minutes to circumnavigate the Earth.'

'We're going ever so fast!'

'Mummy!' called Jemima. 'That was Mummy's voice.'

'Big Ben is officially supersonic.'

'Congratulations,' said Jeremy.

'Jemima, I do hope you're behaving yourself. No arguments, I hope.'

Jemima assured her mother that there were no arguments. She pushed herself in front of Jem, so that Jeremy wouldn't see that she had brought a stranger into the lab.

'We saw the sun rise over Japan. And then we saw it again over the Himalayas. Such a nuisance that we don't have a camera,' said Mimsie.

'Dinosaurs!'

'Little Harry!' cried Jem.

Jeremy looked up at the sound of Jem's voice. His eyes narrowed but he said nothing yet. All his attention was on the radio.

Mimsie was telling the children not to worry. 'We've got plenty of your father's patent whistling sweets. Listen.' There was a long, fruity blast on a whistle. 'They're keeping our spirits up. Only thing we might get short of soon is oxygen.'

'Listen carefully,' said the Commander. 'This is what you need to do. Our plan was to land Big Ben safely back in her historic parking space next to the Houses of Parliament. Sadly, when we got to Big Ben we found that a frightful little man with red hair was stealing our retro-engine. So at the moment we can't slow down. Not to worry. There's a spare set of retro-engines in Chitty's boot. All you have to do is start the old girl up, get her airborne. We'll rendezvous over the English Channel. I'll open Big Ben's clock face. You drop the retro-rockets over the side. I'll fit them. Everything will be tickety-boo—'

'But—'

'We can keep Big Ben up in the air as long as the antigravity paint lasts.'

'But—'

'Sorry, old sport, can't hear you. You're breaking up. Don't worry. We'll be back over England in another one hundred and eighty-eight minutes. Speak then.'

There was a crackle of static.

Then radio silence.

Jeremy looked at Jemima.

Jemima looked at Jeremy.

They both looked at the Cube of Metal That Had Once Been Chitty Chitty Bang Bang.

They didn't say a word, but Jem knew what they were thinking. That cube of metal was once an engine full of hope. Now it was a cube of hopelessness.

'You should have told Father,' said Jemima. 'You should have told him that there is no Chitty Chitty Bang Bang. Maybe he would have had an idea.'

'You tell him,' snapped Jeremy. 'Tell him that we let them crush the most famous car in the world.

Tell him he's trapped in supersonic Big Ben and it's all our fault.'

'It's not really your fault,' said Jem.

'This lab is top secret,' said Jeremy. 'You shouldn't even be in here. Please leave. We're very busy.'

'Busy doing what?' said Jem. 'You don't have any ideas.'

'If we did,' said Jeremy, 'they would be top secret. Go now. This is none of your business.'

'My little brother is up there with them,' said Jem. 'Of course it's my business.'

'What are we doing to do?' sobbed Jemima.

'I will think of something, if I get some peace and quiet.'

'Fine,' said Jem. 'I'll get out of your top-secret lab.'

But when he got to the doorway, Jem looked back at the two children, standing in the dark, next to the silent radio, and he couldn't leave.

'You know,' he said, pointing at the Cube of Metal That Had Once Been Chitty Chitty Bang Bang, 'we can fix this. This is not just a car. This is Chitty Chitty Bang Bang. She's not a collection of wires and gaskets and bolts and nuts. She's Chitty Chitty Bang Bang. Do you think Chitty Chitty Bang Bang will allow herself to be reduced to a chunk of scrap? When all her different pieces were scattered all over the world, we found them and fixed her. When the people in El Dorado took her completely to pieces, we put her back together. We'll fix Chitty Chitty Bang Bang.'

'Oh!' said Jemima, her eyes aglow. 'Do you really think so?'

'I really do,' said Jem. He really did.

'Fix her,' said Jeremy, 'how?'

And although he really did think they could fix her, he really, really could not imagine how. He had to say something so he said, 'My dad will do it.'

Terrible things were happening in Dad's life. His younger son was thundering around the skies in a tower that was designed to stay still for hundreds of years.

His family was stranded fifty years in the past.

His car had been stolen by an evil supervillain who dreamed of one day ruling the world. England had lost the only World Cup she had ever won.

But when he saw Commander Pott's Secret Laboratory he forgot to worry about any of these things. 'Just look at this place,' he said, his eyes devouring the shelves of gadgets, gizmos, valves and springs; the walls covered in diagrams and formulae, calculations and sketches; the benches littered with tools and equipment. Best of all, there was the Commander's old Navy hat and binoculars hanging on the back of the door. 'Now this,' he sighed, 'is the workshop of a genius. This is where he built a car that could travel in time and under the sea . . .'

'Don't forget the square potatoes and edible records,' added Jemima.

'And antigravity paint.'

'This . . .' breathed Dad, 'well, I could live like this. Standing here, I feel like I could do anything.'

'But could you,' said Jemima, her voice full of hope, 'turn that into a car again?'

Dad looked at the Cube of Metal That Had Once Been Chitty Chitty Bang Bang. Up close, like this, it looked more solid, somehow more cube-y and less car-like, than it had in the scrapyard. The word '**NO**' popped into Dad's brain in very large bold letters, swiftly followed by the phrase 'NOT IN A MILLION YEARS' in bright flashing neon.

'Yes,' said Dad. 'I believe I can.'

'It's an unusually complicated car,' warned Jeremy, 'and you do have unusually fat fingers.'

Dad screwed up his eyes and tightened his fists. Nothing was more guaranteed to get him going than a disparaging reference to his fingers.

'Jeremy!' gasped Jemima. 'You know it's wrong to make personal comments.'

'Those fingers might be fat,' said Mum, 'but they are stuck to the hands of the world's greatest mechanic.'

'Thank you,' said Dad. He stood over the cube. 'Think of Chitty as a sheet of beautiful paper. Imagine that someone – some fool – has screwed that piece of paper up and thrown it into the bin. All we have to do is take that piece of paper and smooth it out.'

'Of course!' said Jemima. 'It's simple!'

'Except,' hummed Lucy, 'a piece of paper doesn't have any moving parts. Which is why uncrumpling a piece of paper is different from uncrumpling a carburettor.'

'It'll just take a bit longer, that's all.'

A rain of radio static burst into the room.

'Big Ben calling Kent, Big Ben calling Kent. This is Big Ben. Do you read us, Kent?'

'Yes, Daddy,' shouted Jemima, who had got to the radio set first.

'Oh dear. We were sort of hoping you wouldn't be there – that you'd be on your way to meeting us.'

'Gosh! Have one hundred and eighty-eight minutes gone already?'

'Sticky thing is, we seem to be losing height. We were at twenty thousand feet earlier. Now we're down at eighteen thousand.'

'Never fear, Commander,' bawled Dad. 'We'll save you!'

'Who on earth is that? Jemima, have you let a stranger into my top-secret laboratory?'

'No, these people are from . . .'

But she was drowned out by a storm of static. Behind it they could just hear Mimsie's faint voice calling, 'Be good, children. See you in one hundred and eighty-eight minutes.'

'Actually it'll be quicker than that,' said Lucy. 'As you lose height, the distance round the Earth gets smaller. So they're going to crash earlier than you think.'

Everything went quiet.

'They're losing height,' said Jeremy.

'They're going to crash,' said Jemima.

'I didn't hear Little Harry,' said Mum, biting her lip.

'So sad,' said Lucy, 'being able to hear their voices when we all know that they are doomed.'

'Jem, Jeremy,' barked Dad, 'it's time for action. Let's uncrumple this car.' He'd put the Commander's Navy hat on and was standing with his hands behind his back like a sea captain. 'Lucy, Jemima, put the kettle on. We're going to need lots of tea.'

'Do what?' shrieked Lucy. 'You want *me* to make *tea*?'

'What a lovely idea.' Jemima smiled. 'Would you like some sandwiches too?'

'Good thinking,' said Dad.

'You've only been in the 1960s for one day,' yelled Lucy, 'and already you've turned into a raving sexist!'

'Dad seems to have everything in hand.' Mum took Lucy gently by the elbow. 'Let's leave him and the boys to it and make that tea, shall we? Jemima, where is the kitchen?'

Jemima led them out of the lab and across the farmyard towards the house, but as soon as they were out of sight Mum said, 'We need to act fast. Dad will restore Chitty to her former glory, but not in time to save Little Harry and your parents. We need a plane. Do you have a plane?'

'A plane? No, we don't have a plane. We don't even have a television.'

'We don't need a plane,' said Lucy.

'What?'

'The Commander invented antigravity paint, remember. All we need is a car. We can cover it in antigravity paint and rendezvous with them over the Channel. If we can get close enough, they can jump out of Big Ben into the car and then let Big Ben crash into the sea.'

'Daddy would never let Big Ben go to the bottom of the sea! At least not without him. A captain always goes down with his ship. Even if it's a clock.'

'What about Little Harry?' gasped Mum.

'Oh. He wouldn't let a baby go to the bottom of the sea either. So . . . I don't know . . . I'm all confused.'

'We'll sort out your confusion later,' said Lucy. 'Meanwhile, have you got a car? The bigger the better. It'll make it easier for them not to miss when they jump, if it's a really big car.'

'Only Chitty. We didn't even have bicycles until last summer. We had to make them ourselves out of scrap.'

'Scrap! Of course!' shouted Mum.

Bucklewing Corner – that graveyard of fast cars – was just a short scramble away through the trees and down a gravel slope. Before they even got there they could hear the gigantic car crusher chomping away, gobbling up cars and spitting out little metal boxes at the far end of the main avenue. Last time they'd seen Bucklewing Corner – just a few hours earlier – it was packed with great herds of broken cars – piled one on top of the other, leaning against each other, happily rusting in the English summer rain. Now, under the floodlights, they saw a wide, carefully mown lawn studded with daisies.

'Where are all the cars?' wailed Mum.

'Crushed,' said Lucy, 'and then tidied away.' She pointed to a wall of metal boxes, six high, running the whole length of the main avenue. A painted sign hung from the trees. It read:

Bucklewing Gardens
World's Neatest and Grooviest
Scrap Metal Dealer.

'He's crushed all the cars,' realized Mum. 'What are we going to do?'

'Duck!' yelled Jemima.

'How will that help . . . oh!'

Wind and noise whirled round Mum's head. There was a whiff of petrol. She curled up into a little ball and looked up just in time to see some kind of van fly over her and bellyflop into the field just a few feet ahead. The driver's door opened and a skinny brown-skinned man stumbled out. He looked at the van, then at the hedge behind him. He was trying to figure out where the road had gone. Like hundreds of drivers before him he had miscalculated Bucklewing Corner and come hurtling through the hedge.

'Are you all right?' said Mum, rushing to help him.

'Quite all right, thank you,' said the driver. 'Thank you. I just need my mummy, that's all.' Then he walked unsteadily away.

'Is he going to be OK?' asked Jemima.

But neither Mum nor Lucy answered. They were staring at the camper van in front of them.

'How can this have happened?' asked Mum. 'It can't be . . . is it?'

In front of them was a 1966 VW Samba Bus – the classic split-window model.

'What is it?' asked Jemima.

'It's a 1966 VW Samba camper van – the classic split-window model,' explained Lucy.

'And we're in 1966 so this car is brand new.' It was bright blue. Its paintwork was flawless and glossy, its windows shining, its tyres as black as liquorice. 'That car,' said Mum, 'is our car.' She took a step towards it and breathed on it as if she wasn't quite sure that it was real. 'Fifty years from now Mr Tooting will lose his job at Tiny Parts for Big Machines – they will say his fingers are too fat.

I will cheer him up by going out and buying this very car. It will be an old wreck by then – cast aside, forgotten about – but he will fix it. He'll make it as good as new.'

'Though sadly he will call it Sneezy,' put in Lucy.

'And that will be the beginning of our adventures. We will fly this car over the Atlas Mountains and across the Sahara Desert. And now we're going to use it to save Little Harry.'

'And Mummy and Daddy.'

Back in the Commander's secret laboratory, Jeremy fished a Swiss Army knife out of his pocket and wedged it between two folds of Chitty's crumpled chassis.

'Aren't you going to help?' he said to Jem.

'I don't have a knife,' said Jem.

'You don't have a knife?' gasped Jeremy, who had never before met a boy who didn't have his own knife.

'You don't have a knife?' said Dad.

'No,' said Jem. 'You wouldn't ever let me have one.' But Dad was already handing him a screwdriver and saying, 'Jeremy, show Jem how to do it.'

'It's OK, thanks,' muttered Jem. 'I can do it.'

The two boys worked on in silence, peeling strips of twisted metal back until a sprig of metal petals bloomed from the side of the block. Jem peered down into the gap.

'Dad,' he called. 'Bring a torch.'

'I've got a torch,' said Jeremy, taking one out of his pocket. 'Don't you have a torch?'

'No, I don't. That's why I asked for one. Shine it down there. Into the hole. What do you see?'

'Something shining. And sharp. And pointy.'

'Do you know what it is?'

'Yes. It's a shiny sharp pointy thing.'

'That is the Zborowski Lightning. Chitty's mascot. The plane with the propeller that goes round. That must be its wing tip. Somehow when everything else got crushed, the Lightning isn't even scratched. It's just buried inside.'

'I don't see why that's exciting,' said Jeremy. 'It's just a mascot.'

Jem explained that the Lightning was made of an unknown element called Zborowskium which is only found inside a meteorite which crash-landed on the Zborowski Estate in 1922. 'It's the Lightning that makes it possible for Chitty to travel through time.'

'I can't help thinking that wheels would be more useful,' said Jeremy sniffily.

'But don't you see? If we can get the Lightning out,' said Jem, 'we could . . .'

He never had the chance to finish his sentence. The door of the secret laboratory burst open.

'Ah,' said Jeremy. 'Tea at last.'

'Oh how embarrassing. We forgot the tea!' said Jemima. 'But we've got something else. Come and see . . .'

The split windscreen of the 1966 Samba van glinted like a pair of laughing eyes. 'Sneezy!' cried Dad. 'Is it really Sneezy?!'

'It's really our old camper van,' said Lucy. 'Just don't call her Sneezy.'

'She's going to help us rescue your parents,' said Mum to Jeremy.

'A foreign car!' said Jeremy. 'Father will never agree to being rescued by a foreign car.'

'Commander Pott invented antigravity paint,' explained Lucy. 'We know that this car is air-worthy because we have already flown it over the Atlas Mountains. So why don't we just spray her with antigravity paint, float her into the path of Big Ben and rendezvous somewhere near Dover?'

'Perfect,' said Dad. 'This way we don't need Chitty Chitty Bang Bang at all.'

It might have been a coincidence, but when he said this, there was a deafening clang as a big lump of metal fell off the Cube of Metal That Had Once Been Chitty Chitty Bang Bang.

Dad was already sitting behind the wheel. 'Open those laboratory doors wide,' he called. 'I'll back her in and we'll get to work with the antigravity spray.'

'Seems a shame to spoil her paintwork,' said Mum.

'You only need to apply the antigravity paint to the parts closest the ground,' said Jemima. 'The tyres.'

Jem wasn't listening to any of them. Like an empty petrol tank filling up with petrol, his heart filled up with memories of the days that he and Dad had spent piecing together this very vehicle from a jigsaw of broken parts, how they had fixed her so well that she had flown through mountain passes and over desert oases. He remembered the deafening roar of her engine the first time they took her out on the road. How people had stared at them. How proud Jem had been, sitting in the front passenger seat with the road map open on his knee and Dad letting him navigate.

'Look out!'

Something went crunch.

Dad slammed on the brakes.

'You've crashed it!' howled Jeremy.

'Oh no!' wailed Jemima. 'Now you've ruined everything. How are we going to rescue our parents now?'

Dad pulled on the handbrake and rushed to the back of the van. He had crashed into the Cube of Metal That Had Once Been Chitty Chitty Bang Bang. The sharp metal petals must have cut into the camper van's electrics. Lightning sparks flashed. Thunderous clouds of smoke whirled. The air crackled.

'It's going to explode!'

Dad jumped back behind the wheel. If the van catches fire, it might explode and kill us all, he thought. If I can drive it into the lake, maybe the fire will go out. He sped out of the doors.

'Dad, don't!'

But the van did not catch fire.

It did not explode.

Dad had only driven it forward a few feet before he realized that the sparks were not coming from the van. They were coming out of the Cube of Metal That Had Once Been Chitty Chitty Bang Bang. And sparks were not all that was coming out of the cube. The pieces of metal that had been crunched and folded into each other unfolded.

They stretched out, relaxed and spread, like a flower emerging from a bud.

First a lovely chrome bumper rose up like a stem, next a pair of doors opened out of the sides like leaves and the great brass Klaxon uncurled like a tendril.

'It's obvious really,' said Dad. 'Putting the van into reverse, while it's in contact with the Lightning, has made it reverse time. So it's now reversing the crushing.'

Tyres plumped up like great pumpkins. The radiator grew straight and tall as a row of peas. The gleaming split windscreen blossomed.

A pair of fabulous headlights popped out and lit up. Chitty Chitty Bang Bang was awake.

'Excellent,' smiled Jeremy, yanking open her boot. 'The retro-rockets are here and shipshape. All we need now is the antigravity paint and a paint gun.'

Pott's Patent Antigravity Paint
Instructions
(Please Read Carefully Before Use)

- Paint works by reversing the force of gravity.
- Apply paint to any part of the object that might be in direct contact with the ground (e.g. soles of shoes).
- In the case of applying paint to footwear, take care to tie laces first.
- In the case of a large object (e.g. rocket or missile), ensure that there are no overhead obstructions before applying the paint. After applying the paint stand well back.

Warning: Antigravity effects will wear off if paint is scuffed, scraped, chipped or otherwise damaged

'Big Ben is losing height,' explained Jeremy. 'She's in grave danger of crashing. When we rendezvous with her we'll spray her with the antigravity paint. That'll push her back up into the sky and give Father a bit more time to fix the retro-rockets.'

'Good thinking,' gasped Jemima, who had

already struggled over with three big pots of paint. 'Would you like me to make you a sandwich after this?'

'No, thank you,' said Jeremy. 'Mr Tooting, I'm sorry for what I said about your fat fingers. You fixed Chitty Chitty Bang Bang, even if you did it by accident.'

'Thank you, Jeremy,' said Dad. 'Now let's go and save Little Harry. And your parents and Big Ben.'

He climbed into Chitty's driving seat. Jem went to sit next to him, the way he always used to, but Jeremy had climbed in already. Jem stood back, waiting for Dad to say, 'No, you go in the back, stranger. I need my navigator.' But he didn't say that. Instead he ruffled Jeremy's hair, handed him the road atlas and said, 'Welcome aboard, navigator.'

Jem stood with his hands in his pockets while the others squeezed into Chitty.

'Come on, Jem,' called Jemima, patting the seat beside her. 'Jump in the back with us girls.'

'There's no room,' sulked Jem.

'Of course there is,' said Jemima, practically climbing on to Lucy's knee to make a space.

'Yes, hurry up, Jem,' shouted Dad. 'We've got an iconic London landmark to save.'

'Not to mention Little Harry,' added Mum.

*

'Hello! Hello!' The voice of Commander Pott came crackling over the radio in the lab. 'Big Ben calling Kent . . . Big Ben calling Kent . . .'

This time, though, there was no answer.

Chitty Chitty Bang Bang was already airborne, soaring over the hills and downs, speeding up into the clouds.

6

The first time the Pott family ever flew in Chitty Chitty Bang Bang was the summer of 1964. They'd been heading for the seaside when they got stuck in an August Bank Holiday traffic jam near Canterbury. Chitty had lifted herself into the air and over the miles of overheating cars. She had cruised over the fields of Kent – altitude 500 feet, speed 100 mph – like a steaming green dragon. For fun she had flown once around the spire of Canterbury Cathedral, frightening the crows and jackdaws, before setting down gently on a sun-baked sandbar in the middle of the English Channel. It had been the most thrilling day ever.

The first time the Tooting family had ever flown in her was when she had terrified them all by falling off the White Cliffs of Dover before spreading her wings and taking them all to Paris.

Today's flight did not feel thrilling or terrifying. It felt beautifully familiar and normal. As she slipped into the air Chitty celebrated with two bangs of her exhaust. She saluted the Kentish Downs below with a dip of her wings. Jemima's hair flapped in the wind like a golden pennant. Jeremy's black mop was blown about like a bird's nest in a hurricane.

Jem leaned over the side and looked down at the mashed-potato mountains of fluffy white cloud. He could just make out Chitty's shadow – a black

thumbprint wobbling across the bottom of a cloud valley. It grew to the size of a flag, wrapped in a rainbow halo, waving victory as they skimmed the peak of a cloud mountain. Chitty's shadow seemed to be playing some sort of chase game with them. Running away from the shark-shaped shadow that was closing in on her from behind. Wait a minute . . . what shark-shaped shadow? Why was a swiftly moving shark-shaped shadow coming up behind them? Jem looked back. He was the first to see it.

It was huge, spiky, shining with gold and glass.

The tower of Big Ben was speeding silently towards them.

'Dad! Dive!' he screamed.

'What is it now, Jem?' huffed Dad. 'We're in a hurry.'

'Go left! Or right! Or something!'

'Jem, you're not making any sense.'

Then Jeremy looked in the rear-view mirror. He saw it too. 'Mr Tooting!' he called. 'Behind you!'

Dad looked in the mirror. There was nothing to see there but a mass of bricks. Bricks getting bigger by the second. He pulled on the wheel.

Too late.

There was a crash.

They shuddered.

They shook.

Supersonic Big Ben had run smack into Chitty Chitty Bang Bang's rear.

7

The second it hit, the clock tower seemed to scatter into a thousand different components. Windows, bricks, doorways all veered off in different directions. Exactly like a flock of starlings that seems like a dense black ball one minute, then explodes into a thousand separate fluttering birds. For a moment Chitty Chitty Bang Bang was hanging in the air, in the middle of a vast exploded diagram of the tower of Big Ben.

They finally heard Big Ben itself – the deep, sonorous *dong* of the greatest bell on Earth, rolling around the clouds, flooding in from all directions. They had not heard the bell before because of course, being supersonic, Big Ben was travelling faster than its own sound. The ringing had had to catch up with the bell.

Then everything happened at once. The bricks

and windows flew back together again. Chitty Chitty Bang Bang fell like a stone. A strange, tingling breeze blew right through Jem, as though his cells were jumping away from each other, just as the bricks of the tower had done.

'Daddy! Mummy!' called Jemima. But the breeze blew all her words in different directions.

It blew the clouds too – so hard and so fast that it seemed as if they were passing through the bodywork of Chitty Chitty Bang Bang, and through the heads of her passengers.

The sky went dark.

The sky went bright again.

It was cold.

It was hot.

It felt as if days and nights, winters and summers were flickering by.

'What's happening?' said Dad.

'I think we just saw a time splash,' said Lucy.

'A what?'

'Surely you've felt it. When you travel in time you get a kind of breeze blowing between your cells. That's because the river of time flows through your body just like blood does. Obviously it's different if you're a ninety-six-metre tower rather than a human being. Each individual brick in the tower is a moment in its life. When the tower made contact with the

Chronojuster, all the moments splashed out of the tower's time river. Then when the Chronojuster had gone, they all flowed back together again.'

'That's really interesting, Lucy,' said Dad. 'So you're saying we just drove right through the middle of the tower of Big Ben without so much as a scratch.'

'Yes.'

'Scratch-free crashing – my favourite kind of driving! But hang on, why are we rapidly losing height?' Dad had been so interested in Lucy's explanations that he hadn't noticed the strange feeling in his stomach or the wind howling round his ears.

'It's because we're plummeting to our doom,' yelled Mum.

They dropped from . . .

Very High to . . .

Really High to . . .

High-ish to . . .

Up in the Clouds to . . .

Under a cloud . . .

Dad screwed up his eyes.

There was a rattle of metal.

A shatter of glass.

'Now are we dead?' asked Dad, with his fingers over his eyes.

8

Dad opened his fingers a smidgeon and peeped out of the car. They had landed safely. Safely for Chitty, that is; not safely for the racing car on top of which she had landed. It was squashed like a bug. A young man was clambering out, waving at them as he ran away. Inexplicably he seemed to be smiling even though his car was crushed.

'Everyone all right?' asked Mum.

The Pott twins were staring back up at the sky, trying to spot Big Ben. But the sky was empty.

'What happened? What's that whining noise?' said Jem. It sounded like the noise a supercharged four-litre mosquito might make as it dive-bombed the back of your neck. But it wasn't a supercharged four-litre mosquito. It was a supercharged four-litre sports car. A Bentley Blower, painted racing green just like Chitty, thundered past Chitty Chitty Bang Bang, blasting her with smoke and dust. Jem glimpsed the glint of goggles as the driver glanced back at them, probably trying to figure out how a huge aerocar came to be parked on top of another car.

Another racing car roared by – a Mercedes, its great bonnet curved down towards its radiator, like a great hound chasing a scent.

Now came a Bugatti, bellowing like a war elephant.

'I think we may have landed in the middle of a race,' said Dad. 'Chitty never could resist a . . .' He didn't finish the sentence. Chitty Chitty Bang Bang slithered off the roof of the crushed car, flopped on to the track and leaped forward.

'No, Chitty, please,' moaned Dad, pushing his foot down on the brake. 'No racing. The word today is *save Little Harry*.' Chitty Chitty Bang Bang's engines laughed loud and long. Somehow Dad had stamped on the accelerator instead of the brake.

Up ahead, the racing cars in the pack were jockeying for position as they powered into a bend. Chitty did not try to move to the outside. She did not try to take them on the inside. She blazed up to the bumper of the Bugatti, headlights glaring, Klaxon blaring. When the car tried to wiggle out of her way, she slithered up alongside and shouldered it clear off the track.

'Sorry! Sorry!' yelled Dad, still trying to gain control of Chitty. Her front wheels were now parallel with the back wheels of the Mercedes. They were so close that Jem could hear the jabber of its furious pistons. Dad tried to move Chitty over, to give the other driver room, but somehow when he tried to steer left, Chitty's nose swung sharp right and she smacked the Mercedes out of the way.

The next bend was different. It was not just a flat curve. The track tipped almost sideways as it ran over a steep bank. The car ahead of them – the racing-green Bentley – sped towards it. At the top of the bank it leaped into the air so high that they could see a wedge of blue sky between its undercarriage and the road. It clunked back on to the track and whizzed off.

It was, Jem thought, actually quite cool. He wished he was in the front with Dad, telling him when to speed up and slow down.

'Foot down, Mr Tooting!' roared Jeremy. 'And brake a bit now . . .' He was so calm, as though he went motor racing every afternoon after lunch.

'Oh the futility of it all,' sighed Lucy, examining her nails. 'We'll all be mangled in a meaningless motor race. Is there anything less dignified than alliteration?'

'I can't look,' squealed Jemima, covering her eyes.

Chitty Chitty Bang Bang steamed into the elbow of the bend, soared into the air, then landed right on the Bentley's bumper. Sparks flew. Chrome clashed against chrome.

'Go, Dad! Faster!' yelled Jem. 'We can win this!'

'Do you think so?' Dad gunned the accelerator. Two tonnes of Bentley skipped into the air, somersaulted like a metal bunny rabbit and crashed into the hay bales.

'Look out!'

Dad had taken his eyes off the track to see what had happened to the crashed car. Now he saw some kind of hut right on his racing line.

Wood splintered.

Glass broke.

The hut collapsed around them.

Chitty stalled in a cloud of smoke and splinters.

'Remarkable stability and phenomenal speed.' A man in a blue overall emerged from a shattered window frame. 'And the brakes . . . 120 mph to a dead stop in no time at all. What kind of car is this?'

'She's a Paragon Panther,' said Jeremy. 'The only one ever built.'

'Really? Are you sure? I seem to have seen her somewhere before.'

'You saw her in a painting,' said Lucy. 'The one that's hanging around your neck.'

'Good heavens!' said the man in the overall. 'You're right.' A framed oil painting had crashed on to his head when Chitty smashed the roof in. It showed a racing-green Paragon Panther crossing the winning line at a glamorous racetrack.

Dad read the inscription on the back aloud:

Chitty Chitty Bang Bang, driven by Count Zborowski, winning the Lightning Handicap, 1922. Shortly after this portrait was painted, the car went completely mad and smashed up the timing hut.

'That's the Count?' said Lucy, taking a closer look at the picture. 'That's not much of a likeness.'

'How could you possibly know?' asked the man in the overall.

'I met him,' said Lucy, 'in New York.'

'But you can't have done. He died in 1924.'

'I don't want to talk about it,' said Lucy.

'At least we know why Chitty brought us here,' said Dad. 'She won an important race here in 1922, and she just couldn't resist winning it one more time.'

'What did we win?' asked Jeremy. 'What was the name of the race? Is there a trophy?'

'Today,' said the man in the overall, 'was not a race. Today was a mystery. A mix-up. An accident waiting to happen.'

The driver of the green Bentley was limping towards them, his face drawn and weary, his eyes cast down. Oh no, thought Jem, he's going to fight Dad for crashing into him. Behind him, battered and bruised, came the Mercedes driver, and behind her the driver of the car they'd crushed.

Jem got ready to run and hide.

'Quick!' said Jeremy, pulling a catapult out of his pocket. 'Grab your catapult.'

'I haven't got a catapult,' admitted Jem.

'You've got no catapult!?' gasped Jeremy.

'Are you the driver of this magnificent machine?' asked the man from the green Bentley.

'In a way,' said Dad. 'Sometimes it seems like she's got a mind of her own. I'm so sorry about—'

'Don't apologize,' said the woman from the Mercedes. 'You saved my sanity. I was going crazy out there.'

'Me too,' said the Bugatti driver, shaking Dad's hand.

'We've been going round and round out there for hours.'

'We didn't mean to have a race. We were just looking for a parking space.'

'Mmmmmm.'

'We're the Essex Vintage Automobile Club. This was supposed to be our annual picnic. A nice day out at this historic racetrack. The car park was full so we nosed around a bit, and the next thing we knew . . .'

'Our cars were whizzing around the track. Round and round. We were getting dizzy. It seemed to be going on forever.'

'Horrible feeling whizzing around a racetrack, trapped in a car you can't control.'

'Can't figure out what happened,' said the Mercedes driver. 'I'd had a bit of trouble with the camshaft. But nothing like this. I'm just very grateful that you came along to rescue us.'

'Oh, please don't mention it,' said Dad.

'He's always rescuing people,' explained Mum. 'Rescuing people and fixing things, it's what he does. He's sort of a mixture of a superhero and a very good mechanic.'

'Terrific driver too,' said the man in the blue

overall. 'Do you realize that you just drove the fastest lap ever recorded here?'

'No, really?' said Dad. 'It was nothing. Can I have it in writing?'

'Do we get a trophy?' asked Jeremy again.

'Pardon me for asking,' said Jemima, 'and excuse me for interrupting, but really have you all gone stark staring mad?! We're supposed to be trying to rescue my parents and find Big Ben! Did I miss something? Have we now decided to stop off for a jolly little race?'

'Sorry,' said Jeremy. 'Races are so exhilarating, you do tend to forget . . .'

'Can we please get back up in the air?'

'Yes, of course,' said Dad, sweeping the broken glass from Chitty's bonnet and dragging the splintered woodwork out from under her bumper.

'If you could just move the wall aside,' said Dad, 'we'll get ready for take-off.'

'I think you may be just a little bit too late,' said Lucy.

'How do you mean?'

'The cars in the race – they may be old-fashioned, but look at the drivers; what are they doing?'

'They're calling for help on their . . . oh . . . on their mobile phones.'

'Exactly. We're not in 1966 any more. This is the twenty-first century.'

'We're in the future!' said Jemima.

'It's the future for you,' said Lucy. 'This is the present for us.'

'If we're in the future,' said Jemima, 'then whatever was about to happen to Daddy and Mimsie . . .'

'Has already happened,' said Lucy. 'In fact, it happened fifty years ago.'

Jeremy and Jemima and Mum instinctively looked up through the broken roof of the hut into the sky.

'Little Harry,' whispered Mum.

'When we bumped into Big Ben, the impact must have knocked the Chronojuster,' said Dad. 'Don't worry. I'll give it a pull now and we'll be back in 1966 in eeeehhhh, ohhhhh, grrrrr . . . No. It's stuck. Never mind. We'll go back to our house and I can work on it in my workshop. Drat this car. Whenever you set off to go somewhere, she takes you somewhere else. She may be beautiful, but she can't be trusted.'

No, thought Jem to himself, as he jumped out to turn the hand crank, the thing about Chitty is that you can always trust her. She's brought us here for a reason. We just don't yet know what it is.

As Jem settled down next to Lucy she whispered, 'Does this race remind you of anything?' It certainly did. He and Lucy had once been trapped in cars that would not stop going round and round a racetrack, when they were on Tiny Jack's yacht, Château Bateau.

'Yes,' said Jem so softly that only she could hear. 'It's definitely Tiny Jack's doing. He must be somewhere near.'

They both shuddered. But neither of them said anything to the others.

'The interesting question,' said Lucy, 'is how did he do it? When he did it to us, we were on his yacht, on his racetrack, in his cars. To take control of all the racing cars on a track, that's a lot more impressive . . .'

'And more dangerous and more evil.'

'That's what I meant. Imagine if he does it on the motorway.'

The route to Basildon lay mostly along the famous M25 motorway. The Pott children sat in silence, thinking about their parents. Jem sat thinking about how terrible it would be if Tiny Jack took control of all the cars on the motorway. Lucy sat thinking about Little Harry. 'If he did survive whatever happened to supersonic Big Ben,' she said, 'he would be fifty-three years old now.'

'Thank you, Lucy.'

'It's strange to think that somewhere out there—'

'That's enough, Lucy.'

'This motorway,' said Jeremy. 'Where does it go? The sun was straight ahead of us to start with, then it was on our right and now it's moving over to the left. Are we going round in circles?'

'Yes, we are. Well spotted. It's a circular motorway. It goes all the way round London, so people don't have to drive through it.'

'Why on earth would anyone want to go round London instead of through it? London is the most exciting city on Earth,' said Jemima.

'Because there are so many cars,' explained Mum.

'Daddy said cars would be extinct by 1979, all except Chitty, who is an immortal masterpiece.'

'Yes,' said Jeremy, looking around. 'Are you sure this is the future? Where are the jet packs and the antigravity boots?'

'They haven't been invented yet.'

'Yes, they have. Daddy invented them. And

antigravitational houses that could float up above the clouds on overcast days. And why are people doing their own shopping? Why aren't their robots doing it for them?'

'We do have robots,' said Lucy, 'but they're not as exciting as you might think. They're mostly building even more cars. There hasn't been a lot of progress in the field of personal transport.'

'We've got the Internet though,' said Dad, so proudly that the Pott children got the impression that he had invented it himself.

'The what?'

'It's a kind of invisible global network that allows people all over the world to show each other photographs of amusing cats,' explained Mum. 'Look! There's World of Leather! And Basildon Services!'

But the Pott children weren't listening. The more they drove around the motorway, the quieter they became. Jem knew what they were thinking. He was thinking the same thought himself. It was this: if the world was not full of Commander Pott's brilliant inventions, that could only mean one thing – that something terrible had happened to the Commander and Mimsie before they could tell the world about them.

9

Soon they were parked outside the Tootings' little terraced house in Zborowski Terrace.

The moment they stepped out on to the pavement, the automatic front door swung open and its electronic voice squeaked, 'Do come in. The kettle is on.'

'No matter what, it's nice to be home,' Mum sighed. Everywhere was neat and tidy and smelling of fresh air and clean laundry.

'Wait a minute . . .' said Mum. 'Our house isn't normally neat and tidy and doesn't normally smell of fresh air and clean laundry.'

'No,' said Lucy. 'Last time we were here, we had the Christmas tree up. The place was full of tinsel and cards because Tiny Jack fooled us into thinking it was Christmas.'

'Always Christmas and never winter,' remembered Mum.

They stood listening to the empty house. Someone had been in and tidied up. Maybe they were still there. As they stood, thinking and listening, they began to notice other little changes about the place. The map of the world that Dad had won for punctuality when he was at school was now elegantly framed and mounted on the wall. The cups that Lucy had won for dancing when she was a little girl were arranged along the mantelpiece. School photographs that had languished forgotten in drawers were now gleaming in frames.

'Tiny Jack has been back,' said Dad.

'This is still our home,' said Mum. 'Moving a few pictures around doesn't change that. I'm not going to be frightened in my own house. Children, you must be starving. You haven't eaten a thing in fifty years. I've brought some of Commander Pott's square potatoes with me. I'll make some chips.'

Seeing Mum slicing potatoes filled the others with confidence. This was their home, and they were not going to let Tiny Jack make them feel uncomfortable.

'Come on,' said Dad. 'Let's see if we can't shift that Chronojuster.'

'OK,' said Jem.

'Actually I was talking to Jeremy,' said Dad. 'He knows the car better than any of us.'

'Right-ho,' said Jeremy. 'Got any oil?'

'There's some WD-40 in the cupboard. Jem, go and get it for Jeremy.'

Feeling sad, Jem got the can of oil and handed it to Jeremy. Then he went to his room for a lie-down.

'Has anyone got a pen and paper? I like to scribble when I'm feeling tense,' said Jemima.

'Why don't you take Jemima up to your room, Lucy, and do some drawing?'

'No, thanks,' said Lucy. 'I'll bring the pen and paper down.'

She got a drawing pad and pen for Jemima, and then joined Jem in his room. 'That kid,' she hissed. 'She likes to scribble when she's tense.'

'I thought I'd be able to talk to Jeremy about Chitty,' said Jem, 'but he's just . . .'

'So much better than you are at everything.'

'Yeah. Thanks for putting that so clearly.'

'No problem. I'm an intellectual. That's what I do.'

They both lay staring at the ceiling, relishing the comfortable quiet of each other's company.

The door opened. Jeremy looked in. 'Chronojuster's looking a bit better,' he said.

'Great,' said Jem. 'Toilet's that way, if that's what you're looking for.'

Jeremy looked around the room.

'If you're hoping to find a robot that makes your bed or a carpet that does your homework,' snapped Lucy, 'forget it. The future is rubbish – it's official.'

'I see,' said Jeremy, turning dejectedly to leave the room. Jem felt a stab of sympathy. Of course what Jeremy had really been hoping to see was one of his father's inventions. Some memory of what the Commander had done.

'You can look at the Internet if you like,' offered Jem.

But Jeremy had spotted something on the end of the bed. 'You haven't unwrapped all your Christmas presents,' he said, 'even though it's July.'

Jem and Lucy stared at the package. It was a large, immaculately wrapped box.

'Who's it from?'

'No label.'

Jem and Lucy looked at each other, each thinking the same thought. What if this was from Tiny Jack?

'Why don't you open it and see what it is?' said Jeremy, bending down to pick it up.

'Don't touch that!' warned Jem. 'It may contain high explosives.'

'Or poisonous spiders,' added Lucy.

Jeremy reached into his pockets and pulled out a pair of goggles and a set of earplugs.

'You carry blast-proof goggles with you?' said Lucy.

'They're very useful,' said Jeremy. 'For instance . . .' He began to unwrap the present. 'It weighs a ton!' The others put their fingers in their ears and screwed up their eyes.

'Look,' said Jeremy. 'It's just a game.'

It was a board game. A bit like Monopoly, but instead of street names it had the names of exciting places such as the Acropolis, the White House and Mount Everest. On each of these squares was a perfect little model. On the square named Mount Everest was an exquisite little mountain with what looked like real snow on top. Lucy reached out to touch it, then pulled her hand away. 'It's cold,' she said, reaching for the Acropolis, 'and that's hot. What is this game?'

'It's called "Destruction",' said Jeremy, holding up the lid and reading the blurb. 'The game that never ends. Once you start, you just can't stop. Fun, fun, fun." Strange . . .'

'What?' asked Lucy.

'That's exactly what the advertising hoardings said at the racetrack. "Fun, fun, fun" and "Once you start, you just can't stop". I always try to notice the details. It's a kind of game.' His face had turned very pale. He was looking closely at a model of the Tower of London. 'Can you lend me your magnifying glass?' he asked.

'I don't have a magnifying glass,' sighed Jem. 'Or a knife, or a catapult, or a jet pack.'

'There's a zoom facility on my camera phone,' said Lucy pointing her jelly phone at the model of St Pancras.

'What on earth is that?' asked Jeremy.

'It's something interesting about the future,' said Lucy. 'Take a look.'

Jeremy looked into the lens, then turned very solemn. Lucy looked and went solemn too.

What they saw when they looked through the zoom was beautiful, but also terrifying. The model of the Tower of London was perfect in every detail. They could even see bird poo on the ramparts. Even more amazing – they could see a little row of ravens parked on Tower Green.

'Oh!'

One of the ravens – no bigger than a grain of rice – had flapped into the air and was flying. Lucy's hand swung away in surprise so that now they were looking at the top of Everest. The snow on the summit was not still – as it would be on a model. It was whirling around in little gusts, as though there was a wind up there.

'Look at the Acropolis,' said Jeremy. Like the other models, the Acropolis was perfect in every detail, right down to the crowd of tourists – the size of ants – that swarmed around it. The frightening thing was that these tiny tourists were moving. They were pointing and hurrying and gathering together. They were tiny ant-sized people.

'These are not models,' said Jeremy.

'What are they then?'

'Try to pick one up.'

Gingerly Lucy took the model of the Tower of London between her fingers and tried to pick it up. It wouldn't move.

'It's so heavy!' she said. 'It must weigh a tonne.'

'It probably weighs hundreds of tons. You see, my father invented a device called the Miniaturizer. If you point it at a thing and activate it, it sucks all the air out from between that thing's atoms.'

'So it shrinks things.'

'Yes.'

'You see, he wanted Britain to win the Space Race but he knew we couldn't afford to keep building bigger and bigger rockets, and then he had this brilliant idea – what if we just had very small astronauts?'

'So that model of the Tower of London . . .'

'The Tower of London is on your desk.'

'But wouldn't people have noticed if the Tower of London was missing? Or the Pyramids?'

'Maybe they have. Let's go and see the news.'

The children hurried downstairs. Lucy flicked through the channels until she found twenty-four-hour news:

. . . scenes of panic all over Athens today as the Acropolis joins the recent list of famous places and buildings worldwide that have simply disappeared. Greeks woke up today to find nothing but a huge hole where only last night the Acropolis had been. The incident follows a similar incident last week when the celebrated mountain Everest was extracted from the Himalayas like a tooth, leaving nothing but an unsightly cavity . . .

'I suppose it is actually quite stylish,' said Lucy, 'having the actual Acropolis in your bedroom.'

'My father kept the Miniaturizer top secret because he knew that if it fell into the hands of an evil genius it would be the most terrible weapon ever invented. Especially if you don't read the instructions.'

'Well, falling into the hands of an evil genius is exactly what it has done,' said Lucy. 'Tiny Jack has got it.'

On the television, a journalist was interviewing an elderly lady whose whole family had gone on holiday to Greece and had disappeared along with the Acropolis.

'Those poor people,' said Mum, passing round a plate of square chips. 'To think their family is here in our house and we can't help them. Your father was right.'

'About square potatoes?'

'About tidying up after you play. The Tooting family is going to tidy up that game. We're going to put every mountain, every monument, back where it belongs.'

'How are we going to do that?'

'We'll track down Tiny Jack, get this Miniaturizer gizmo back off him. Then we'll just have to maximize all the things he's miniaturized. Perhaps Commander Pott can invent a Maximizer?'

No sooner had she finished speaking than a piercing ring tone shrieked from the jelly phone. Tiny Jack's profile picture grinned up at them from the screen.

'It's him,' whispered Lucy. 'It's Tiny Jack.'

'Give that to me,' commanded Mum.

'Hello, dear Tootings!' cackled Tiny Jack's voice over the speakerphone. 'Are we having fun, fun, fun? Wanna play a game of hide-and-seek?'

'Certainly not,' snapped Mum. 'Why on earth would we play with you? You've abducted Little Harry. You've practically destroyed the Himalayas. You've created panic in Greece and London. You are a very naughty boy.'

'I know. Ha ha ha ha. But naughty boys are more fun.'

'Not in my book. We're not playing any games with you.'

'Ha! You think I care? I'm the greatest car thief in history. I stole Chitty Chitty Bang Bang – the most famous, most expensive, most marvellous car ever built.'

'Hmmm, debatable,' said Lucy.

'*What* was that?'

'Chitty might be the most marvellous, but she's not the most expensive. That's got to be the Apollo Lunar Rover. It cost thirty-eight million dollars.'

There was a trembling silence on the other end of the phone and then the line went dead.

'You certainly told him, Mrs Tooting,' said Jeremy.

'Thank you, Jeremy.'

*

All this time Dad had been working away at the Chronojuster. The problem was that, as he didn't actually know how it worked, it was hard for him to figure out how to fix it.

'We could ask Chitty,' said Jem, when Dad came in for a breather.

'If she could talk.'

'But she does talk in her own way. She flashes up those messages.'

'That's true. Jem, you crank up the engine. Jeremy, want to give me a hand?'

Jem turned the hand crank while Dad and Jeremy sat in the front seat. The engine coughed into life. On the dashboard, dials spun and lights flickered . . . until the message light burned with one steady, insistent word:

'But she doesn't need antifreeze,' said Jeremy. 'She's air-cooled, and besides, it's the height of summer. Maybe the warning light is faulty.'

Another message flashed up:

Then . . .

AND QUICK ABOUT IT!

'Why on earth would a car need de-icer in the middle of summer?' said Jeremy.

'If Chitty Chitty Bang Bang says she wants antifreeze,' said Jem, 'it's probably best to give it to her. I'll go and see if we've got any.'

When Jem hurried through the kitchen, on his way to the shed for antifreeze, Mum and Lucy were still discussing Tiny Jack's phone call. 'You told him, all right,' agreed Lucy, 'but I'm not sure you told him the right thing. After all, we *do* want to find him, don't we? We *are* playing hide-and-seek with him.'

'Oh,' said Mum. 'Yes, we are.'

'But if he was asking us to play hide-and-seek,' said Jem, 'that might be a trap. We have to find him in our own way.'

'Exactly,' agreed Mum.

'So,' said Lucy, 'which way is that?'

'The North Pole,' said Jemima, looking up from her drawing pad.

'What?'

'That's where Mother and Father would have come down when Big Ben landed.'

'How do you know?' said Lucy.

'Simple. I took the speed at which they were losing height, and the speed at which they were travelling and I plotted their trajectory on to this Mercator's projection of the world, using the lines of longitude as my guide . . .'

'That's impressive,' said Mum.

'And surprising,' said Lucy.

'Why surprising?'

'Because I thought . . .'

'You thought I would be bad at maths just because I'm a girl?'

'No, I thought you would be bad at maths because you always act like such a fluffy-headed muppet.'

'I'm not sure what those words mean, but I think what you're saying is that I don't like to be too showy-offy about my brains.'

'Your maths is good up to a point,' said Lucy. 'But there's something you've forgotten.'

'If you're talking about the displacement caused by the centrifugal force of the Earth's rotation, don't worry – I've taken it into account. Having factored that into the equation, I think they came down exactly here . . . Look, someone has written something there already.'

She pointed to the North Pole on the map that

Dad had won for punctuality at school. Someone had indeed already written something there. The word 'Dad'.

'That's funny,' said Jem, leaning over them. 'On the day that Dad lost his job at Tiny Parts for Big Machines, we all sat down and talked about where in the world we'd like to go and then marked it on this map. Lucy said Egypt, Mum said Paris, I said El Dorado, Dad said the North Pole. Dad's the only one who hasn't been to his destination of choice.'

'This is hardly the time to go off on a jaunt,' said Jeremy, who had come in to see what was taking Jem so long.

'But don't you see? Jemima says your parents landed at the North Pole. Chitty is asking for antifreeze. The North Pole is marked on the map. Chitty Chitty Bang Bang is trying to tell us something.'

'Tell us what?'

'She's telling us to go to the North Pole. Everyone, get your coats!'

10

There is no land at the North Pole. Only a constantly shifting cap of ice, floating on the dark Arctic seas.

At the top of the Earth, all the world's lines of longitude meet. So the North Pole is in every time zone at the same time.

What time is it at the North Pole?

It is all the time.

What difference does time make here anyway? The sun rises in March and doesn't set until September. One day lasts half a year.

If ever a place had no need of a clock, this was it.

Yet there is a clock here. A very big clock.

Rising out of the ice is something like a huge inverted icicle. It is the tower of Big Ben. It crash-landed on the ice fifty years ago. It sticks there like a spindle through a humming top. Very slowly the pack ice rotates around it.

Flying low over the pack ice, her big, bold headlights searching through the swirling snow, her wipers valiantly swishing back and forth to keep the windscreen clear, Chitty Chitty Bang Bang is heading for the Pole.

Inside, the Tootings and the Pott children were wrapped up in every jumper, every pair of socks, every coat and every pair of gloves they had been able to lay their hands on before they left Zborowski Terrace. Chitty's great leather hood was stretched above them and fastened to the windscreen. Even so, they were cold. Chitty Chitty Bang Bang had wings, and ejector seats, and tyres that could turn into propellers in the water. What she did not have was heating.

'How do we know we're going the right way?' asked Mum.

'Do you want me to come and sit in the front and read the map?' asked Jem eagerly. 'I could swap places with Jeremy.'

'There's no point,' said Jeremy. 'The map just looks like a blank page. Everything is flat and white.'

'Couldn't you stop and ask directions?' said Mum.

'Stop where? Ask who?' snapped Dad. They were always having this argument.

'The nearest permanent land is called Coffee Club Island,' said Lucy.

'There,' said Mum. 'You'd like a coffee, wouldn't you? I'm sure the people there will know the way . . .'

'It's seven hundred kilometres away,' said Lucy

'Oh,' said Mum. 'Well, never mind, I've got a flask of coffee here.' She produced the flask of coffee. 'I just wish I could be certain we were heading in the right direction.'

'Why not just use your compass?' asked Jeremy.

'Haven't got one,' said Dad.

Jeremy looked at Jem. Jem shrugged. Jeremy tried not to look as if he thought a boy who didn't carry a compass was only one step up from a boy who consistently forgot to wear trousers. He took off his right shoe. 'My compass is embedded in the sole of my shoe. It's another of Father's inventions.' He carefully placed his shoe upside down on top of the gearstick so Dad could see the needle, quivering, pointing northwards over the unrelenting ice.

'Why on earth did you say you wanted to come here?' asked Mum. 'I can see why Lucy wanted to see Egypt, or why Jem wanted to see El Dorado, but this is like very slowly reading a very thick book full of completely blank pages.'

'I just really love penguins,' said Dad.

No one said a word.

'What?' said Dad. 'Why have you all gone quiet?'

'You're going to be very disappointed, Mr Tooting,' said Jemima. 'There are no penguins at the North Pole. They live at the South Pole.'

'Ah . . . But come on. The North Pole. Imagine that. I mean it's north and it's a pole.'

'You do know there's no actual pole there, don't you?' asked Lucy.

'What?' asked Dad, hastily adding that of course he knew that because everyone knew that. 'Why would there be a pole?'

But there was a pole.

Pointing into the polar sky like a huge finger. No sooner had they seen it than they heard it. The tolling of the great bell swept towards them through the unending blizzard as though Big Ben was pleased to see them.

They sped towards it. They circled it once. The warm glow of its clock faces lit them. Dad tried to land alongside the main door but Chitty Chitty Bang Bang had other ideas. As her tyres touched ground, she swung round on her back wheels, driving a vast drift of snow to one side, so that, when she finally stopped, her exhaust pipe was almost touching the frozen door handle of Big Ben. Her engines carried on running, pouring smoke and steam and heat until the ice around the door melted. The Arctic wind pushed it open.

'In we go, children, let's try to keep warm, shall we?' sang Mum.

They dashed inside and pulled the door behind them. It was good to be out of the wind. But now they were in utter darkness, as though they were standing inside a huge column of granite.

It was dark but it was not quiet. The slowly moving pack ice ground against the outside of the building, groaning and creaking. It sounded like some great forsaken giant begging to be let in.

'The word today,' said Dad, 'is *where is the light switch?* The whole tower used to be lit up at night like a big birthday cake.'

'I think you'll find that they plugged those lights

into the main electricity supply,' said Lucy. 'There isn't one here.

'Ah . . . Never mind,' said Dad. 'I'm sure Jeremy has got a box of matches. And a candle.'

A scratch. A splutter. Jeremy held the burning match over his head before lighting the candle. He stepped on to the first of the three hundred and ninety-three steps that led to the top of the tower. No one spoke. They were all thinking the same thing. Big Ben crashed here in 1966. Nearly half a century has passed. There was no food here. No hope of rescue. The passengers must be dead. Somewhere upstairs, almost certainly, lay the skeletons of Commander Pott, Mimsie and Little Harry.

All her life, Lucy had been fascinated by graves and ghosts and skeletons. Now that she was finally standing in a great, Gothic, ice-bound grave, she couldn't remember why. 'Why did we come here?' she asked.

'Chitty Chitty Bang Bang brought us here,' said Jem, taking her hand and giving it a squeeze, 'so somehow it will be all right.'

The three hundred and ninety-three steps of Big Ben snake up the inside of the building, getting steeper as they get higher, curling around a huge empty drop.

Then they stop.

At the top there is usually nothing but a vast, shadowy space where the bell – Big Ben itself – hangs like small planet. Usually. Now that space was filled with wires and pipes and motors. A huge cylinder ran from the ground to the bell chamber. This had been the fuel tank that had powered Big Ben on its flight around the Earth. It had burned so much fuel so quickly that even now, fifty years later, it was still quite warm.

'Hello?' called Dad, though he knew there could be no one there. It just seemed the polite thing to do.

'Hello?' echoed back the caverns and corners of the tower.

The only other sound was the deep, sad creaking of the ice.

'Well, nobody home,' said Dad. 'Let's go.'

'There's a light,' said Jeremy.

'I wish there wasn't,' sighed Dad.

Jeremy climbed the last few steps. There was a shelf, reaching out over the cobwebby void. On it was a tangle of wires. Snared in the wires was some kind of microphone, its head pointing down towards a little black machine. It had a row of big buttons along its front and a glass panel in its belly. Above the keys, glowing and fading, glowing and

fading, was a tiny red light. Next to the machine was a laminated note in spidery handwriting:

Press play.

'What does that mean?' asked Jem.

'Play on the cassette,' explained Jeremy, pointing to the black box.

'What is it? A game?'

'It's a device for recording sound.' Jeremy pressed play.

A wicked little laugh ricocheted around the steps and nooks and crannies.

'Tiny Jack,' said all the Tootings at once.

'Fun, fun, fun,' cackled the voice of Tiny Jack.

'If you are looking for Commander Pott or his wife or my dear friend Little Harry, then . . . HA! HA! FOOLED YOU! They're not here and they never were here! If you think you heard them calling for help as Big Ben crashed . . . that was me!' And with that he did a perfect imitation of the voice of Commander Pott: 'Big Ben to Kent, Big Ben to Kent . . .'

The imitation was so life-like that Jemima whistled. Her whistle blew out the candle.

While Jeremy was relighting it, Tiny Jack did an impersonation of Little Harry saying 'Dinosaurs!'

that was so lifelike Mum gasped, but this time Jeremy moved the candle out of the way in time.

'I sent you those radio messages from the comfort of my luxury yacht! There was never anyone in Big Ben!'

'But if Mummy and Daddy weren't in Big Ben,' said Jemima, 'then where are they?'

'Turn off the tape,' said Jeremy. 'Let's try to do this logically.'

'DO NOT TURN OFF THAT TAPE!' shrieked Tiny Jack from the tape machine. 'YOU LISTEN TO ME NOW. When I was a little boy I was abandoned, left all alone, in New York with nothing but the Diamond As Big As Your Head. The people who did this – I thought they were my friends. I thought maybe they were just playing hide-and-seek. But they weren't. Well, now it's my turn to play hide-and-seek. If you want Commander Pott, or Little Harry or Mimsie, come and get them. In a moment I'll start counting. Those so-called friends were you, the Tooting family. And now it's my turn to abandon you in the middle of nowhere.' He laughed loud and long. 'If you're worried about Commander and Mrs Pott, and Little Harry, don't be! They're all here on Château Bateau, just relaxing and making friends.'

'That's nice,' said Jemima.

'We'd be thrilled if you could join us. But you probably can't.'

'Poor Tiny Jack,' said Mum. 'I hadn't thought about that before. We left him alone in New York. He was just a little boy. We put him back where he belonged. It's the first rule of time travel. Have fun, but put things back where they belong when you've finished. New York was where he belonged. No one belongs on their own.'

'He did have the Diamond As Big As Your Head,' pointed out Lucy.

'I think that makes it worse.'

'EXCUSE ME, ARE YOU LISTENING TO ME? When you pressed play on that tape recorder, you initiated the detonation sequence for a massive bomb which is hidden somewhere in this building and which will blow Big Ben to smithereens on the last stroke of midnight!' He laughed again. 'The fun never stops with Tiny Jack!'

'Ah,' said Dad.

'Oh,' said Mum.

'Counting to a hundred,' said Tiny Jack. 'One . . . two . . . three . . . four . . .'

'Quick! We're about to be blown to smithereens!' said Jem.

'Oh, I'm sure you clever boys will save us,' Jemima said with a smile.

'Don't worry!' said Dad. 'There's no way that the mechanism will still be working after fifty years in the Arctic.'

The words were no sooner out of his mouth than they heard a grinding of gears above their heads. Then silence. Then something went tick. The gears again. Another tick. The clock had started.

'British engineering,' said Jeremy. 'Best there is.'

Tick.

'How long till Big Ben strikes midnight?' asked Jem.

Tock.

'It said five minutes to twelve on the clock,' said Jemima.

Tick.

'Sorry, three minutes . . .'

Tock.

'. . . before we're blown to smithereens.'

11

It's impossible to hurry downstairs with a lighted candle if you need the candle to stay lit. So they went slowly, step by step, with the ticks of the clock filling the air. The slower they stepped, the faster it seemed to tick.

They tumbled out of the door into the Arctic wind.

'We need to get out of here,' yelled Jeremy, 'as quickly as possible.'

'I think we're aware of that,' said Lucy. 'If we don't get blown to bits, we'll freeze to death.'

'Chitty will save us,' said Jeremy.

'Are you sure?' said Lucy, her teeth chattering. 'Take a look at the wheels.'

After her long flight, Chitty Chitty Bang Bang's twenty-three-litre engine had been extremely hot.

When she landed outside Big Ben, the ice beneath her wheels had melted. But in the time it took for the Tootings to get up and down those three hundred and ninety-three steps, that melted ice had frozen again. So the top half of Chitty was sticking out of the snow, like a Flake sticking out of an ice cream, while her wheels and undercarriage were locked in the ice. Her headlights blazed and then faded, then blazed and then faded. It seemed this was the automobile version of keeping warm by blowing on your hands.

'I don't suppose you've got a pickaxe in your pocket?' said Jem to Jeremy.

'No. Sorry.' He was already stabbing away at the ice with his little pocket knife.

'Even if we free the wheels,' said Lucy, 'Chitty will never gain enough traction to drive over the ice.'

'We could try running away really fast,' said Jem.

'When our greatest national icon is being sabotaged?' gasped Jeremy. 'I don't think so.'

The others were huddled in the doorway. It was so cold that it was almost impossible to think any thought apart from 'I'm so cold'. Even the thought 'We're about to be blown sky high by an exploding Big Ben' seemed less important than 'I'm so cold'.

'This is probably silly,' chattered Jemima, 'but what about Daddy's antigravity paint?'

Everyone stared. Everyone could see at once that if they could just free Chitty from the ice in time, and apply the paint quickly enough, she would be up in the air before the explosion. It was such a good idea that they all felt slightly warmer.

'Only goes straight up in air,' said Lucy. Her lips were too cold for full sentences.

'Sails?' chattered Jemima.

'Got duvets,' said Mum. 'Could use.'

'We'll never get wheels free in time,' said Jeremy. His pocket knife had made just a few little pecks in the ice.

Jem ran to the toolbox. He'd had a brilliant idea. 'Stand back, all of you,' he commanded. He had found a can of de-icer. Now he sprayed it on the front passenger wheel. The ice crumbled.

He swept it away with his boot.

'That's amazing,' said Jeremy. 'Can you do it again?'

'Sure.'

Jem de-iced all four wheels while Jeremy fitted a pot of Pott's Patent Antigravity Paint to the paint gun. 'There you go,' he said, offering Jem the nozzle. 'You spray. I'll work the pump. The more paint we get on her, the higher she'll go.'

Jem was pleased and surprised that Jeremy had offered him the fun part of the job. The paint froze into hard little beads almost as soon as it left the nozzle, but it melted again when it touched Chitty's still-warm undercarriage. He sprayed her front wheel arches and her tyres. In a few moments the front end of Chitty Chitty Bang Bang was rising into the air. 'Ga gooo ga!' blared her Klaxon.

She doesn't like that, thought Jem. It's because she's not in control. She likes to be the one in charge.

'Quick!' shouted Jeremy. 'We need to balance her.'

'What if she floats off completely before we can get on board?' asked Jem.

As if the car herself had heard him, a message lit up on the dashboard. From the corner of his eye, Jem caught the faint glow of the warning light.

'Message from Chitty!' he called.

'What does she say?'

(Obviously as Chitty Chitty Bang Bang is a sailing vessel as well as an automobile and flying machine, she has an anchor.) That'll steady her, thought Jem. She'll be happier then.

'All right, all right,' said Jem, swinging himself on board and pressing the anchor release. The anchor plunged itself into the ice, steadying the car. Chitty seemed calmer now. Jem went back to turning her crank handle. Chitty was now floating elegantly just a metre or so off the ground. Her headlamps were level with Jem's eyes. It was the first time in all their adventures that he had been face to face with Chitty, except when crouching down to turn her crank handle.

Suddenly she drifted slightly upwards, swaying like a balloon that's about to drift away. 'Whoa!' called Jem, grabbing her by the bumper and trying to steady her, as though she was a nervous carthorse.

'All aboard,' called Dad. 'And anchors aweigh!' He pulled on the anchor release and the great chain rattled back up into Chitty's undercarriage.

'Hey! Wait for me!' called Jem as the car floated higher. He just managed to grab the hook of the anchor before it disappeared. Jemima reached over and helped him climb over the door and into the seat. The back seat of course. Jeremy, as ever, was in the front.

The Westminster chimes rang out their nursery rhyme tune as though nothing in the world could ever go wrong.

Then Big Ben itself rang.

A single, doom-laden BOING . . .

BOING . . .

The rich Rolls-Royce tone of Big Ben cruised through the howling of the polar wind.

'The stroke of midnight,' Mum gasped.

'Quick, Jem. Jump in!' shouted Dad.

BOING . . .

Chitty was free. Up she rose, not thrusting skyward as he did when her mighty engines were running, but thrust backwards and forwards in the howling wind.

BOING . . .

'Hoist the duvet!' yelled Dad. 'We need to get clear before we crash into the tower wall!'

BOING . . .

Was that the fifth or sixth?

'Hold on, everyone!' Mum had got the duvet in place. She cast it wide. It filled with wind. Chitty Chitty Bang Bang rocketed through the air.

Two seconds later Big Ben was no more than a shrinking pile of snow.

Boing.

Twenty one and a quarter seconds (and three boings) later the whole sky filled with sparks and flames.

Boing.

Big Ben was erupting like a Roman candle – flinging glass and bricks across the ice.

No more boings.

After the thunder of the explosion came a gust of hot air, pushing Chitty further and faster.

'That was close,' said Jem.

'We're saved!' cried Jemima.

'Not quite,' said Lucy. 'Look at the wings.'

A spray of frost was forming on the leading edge of Chitty's wings. They watched in fear as the frost thickened into ice, and the green of those great sweeping wings turned white. Chitty Chitty Bang Bang's mighty bonnet lurched downward, like the carriage of a roller coaster. The white Arctic rushed up to meet them. The ice on Chitty's wings was weighing her down. Dad struggled to keep her in the air.

Jem jumped up. Mum tried to pull him back down. 'Keep calm,' she said. 'I'm sure Dad's got it all under control.'

'I am calm. I just need to . . .'

'You're going to overbalance the car.'

He was trying to climb into the front.

'Jem, this is not the time to argue about who sits where.'

Jem snatched his arm free, reached past Dad and grabbed hold of the Chronojuster's ebony handle. He pushed it forward as far as he could.

A blizzard of stars swarmed around their heads. The polar wind blew straight through their bodies.

'Jem, what are you doing?! Get off!' yowled Dad. 'Get back into the back.'

'He's gone crazy!' yelled Jeremy.

Jem kept pushing and pushing. Nothing would budge him.

'Leave him!' cried Lucy. 'I'm sure he knows what he's doing. Look at the wings.'

The wings that had been white with ice were green again. The car that had been plummeting earthwards was floating, like a feather.

'I remembered Lucy telling me that fifty-five million years ago the North Pole was covered in tropical forest.'

'Of course,' said Lucy, 'the Palaeocene–Eocene Thermal Maximum! Why didn't I think of that?!'

'All we had to do was travel back fifty-five million years to when it was warm, then fly south.'

'That's actually rather brilliant, Jem,' said Jeremy.

'Thank you.'

'No. Thank you.'

'The weather is so lovely,' said Jemima, 'we could take the top off.' Dad pressed the button and Chitty Chitty Bang Bang's leather roof lifted up and retracted. 'We're flying so smoothly. It's almost like swimming.' They took off their gloves and coats and threw them in the back. They rode the thermals of hot air that curled up from the rainforest. They gazed in wonder at the carpet of steaming green jungle below.

'That's the world before it started . . .' Jemima sighed.

'In fact,' said Lucy, 'the world started long before this. Fifty million years is the day before yesterday to a geologist. There are already mammals down there and crocodiles. But,' she added, 'it is the world as it was before anyone made any mistakes.'

Chitty Chitty Bang Bang was moving at the same speed as the tropical breezes, so the air around them felt as still and hushed as the inside of a tent on a summer's afternoon. It was only when they looked down and saw the green blur miles below them that they realized how quickly they were travelling.

'Oh, I could live like this,' Dad said dreamily. 'Just drifting along on the breeze like a massive dandelion seed.'

'Thank you for saving our lives, Jem,' said Jeremy. 'Now can we go and save our parents' lives, please?'

'Where do you want to start?' asked Dad. 'Tiny Jack could be anywhere in space and time, stealing things.'

'He's angry with us for leaving him in New York in 1926,' said Lucy. 'He wants revenge. We don't have to look for him. He'll come looking for us. Let's go home.'

'You left him in New York?' asked Jemima. 'When he was just a little boy?'

'Well, he was from New York, we just put him back where we found him,' said Dad.

'Ah,' said Jemima. 'All the same, it does seem to be a habit of yours to leave little boys behind all over the place. That's how we met Little Harry after all.'

Dad took the handle of the Chronojuster and eased it forward. Lucy leaned over for one last look at the great forest of the Palaeocene–Eocene Thermal Maximum. She could see the great sweep of the coast, and the ice spreading across it like icing. She just had time to think, If I can see the sweep of the coast, doesn't that mean we're unusually high? before the tingle of the time breeze stopped her thinking at all.

When the time breeze stopped blowing through them they knew they were back in the twenty-first century, because when they looked down they could see roads and cities twinkling like fairy lights. The great patches of darkness must be the sea.

'There's something down there,' said Dad, pointing. 'What is it? Like a tiny bird.'

'That's a plane. That's a big plane. A passenger plane. We're higher than a passenger plane.'

'The sky is changing colour,' said Jemima. 'It used to be blue, but now it's going turquoise. Please don't think I'm complaining. I do like turquoise.

But I think turquoise is probably not the colour of air you can breathe.'

'I think you should take us back down now,' said Mum.

'I'm trying,' said Dad. 'But we just keep floating upward.'

'Daddy's antigravity paint really does work very well.' Jemima smiled proudly.

'The only problem with paint,' said Lucy, 'is that you can't turn it off.'

'So where are we going?'

'Well,' said Lucy, 'I don't think we're going to Basildon.'

12

Chitty Chitty Bang Bang rose higher and higher. She passed though ranges of clouds that seemed like mountains. The needle of her altimeter crept across the dial until it couldn't creep any further.

But still they climbed.

They could look down on the cloud mountains now and see them as puffs of white hovering over the wide blue ocean.

And still they climbed.

The air grew thin and ice cold. Breathing in was like inhaling ice cubes.

Still they climbed.

'Not wishing to trouble you,' wheezed Jemima, 'but is anyone else finding it slightly difficult to breathe?'

Chitty Chitty Bang Bang swayed from side to side as if looking for a way down.

But still they climbed.

There was nothing even Chitty could do about the antigravity paint. A message flashed up:

'What on earth is the sun dome?' asked Dad.

Dad followed Chitty's directions and found a little wheel. He turned it, and out of the space where the roof canopy was normally stored rose a great glass dome, which clicked into place just in front of the windscreen.

'We're in a goldfish bowl!' laughed Jemima.

'The toughened glass will help deal with the changes of pressure we're experiencing in our ascent,' said Lucy. 'The dome shape will concentrate the sun's rays and help keep us warm.'

'How super,' said Jemima.

'What about breathing?' asked Jem.

'That hissing sound is the oxygen fountain,' explained Lucy.

Suddenly Chitty was buffeted from side to side. They all clung to their seats.

'Oh no! This must be the thermosphere,' cried Lucy. 'It's going to be incredibly turbulent for the next million feet or so.'

It was like riding in the barrel of a rocket-propelled washing machine. Jemima grabbed hold of the nearest solid thing she could. It was a door handle. The door flew open and for a second she saw what lay beneath them. It was too frightening to describe. She almost passed out and fell out. Jem grabbed the handle and Jemima and pulled the door shut. Seeing the fear on Jemima's face, he avoided looking down. He knew how high they were. He just didn't want to see how high they were.

'Thank you,' shuddered Jemima.

Chitty rocked, shook, rolled, then flipped completely upside down.

Miles below them they saw the great blue disc of Earth.

Then the disc seemed to flex itself, bend itself, puff itself up. It was no longer a disc. It was a ball. A planet.

Inky blackness spilled through the sky.

The blacker the sky became, the bluer and

more beautiful the Earth looked.

Then the blackness sugared itself with stars. Chitty Chitty Bang Bang pulled in her wings, as though she was curling up and settling down in a dear, familiar black velvet chair.

'No! Chitty!' called Jemima. 'Stop her. Her wings are collapsing. We'll fall!'

'I don't think so,' said Lucy. 'We're so high we don't need wings any more. We're in space.'

13

'I'll say one thing for Commander Pott,' said Lucy. 'When he decides to make something antigravity, he makes it really, really antigravity. It would normally take a rocket the size of St Paul's Cathedral filled with fuel to push something as big as Chitty Chitty Bang Bang out of Earth's atmosphere.'

No one said anything. Everyone looked down at the Earth, wishing that it would just stop getting smaller.

'Are we eventually going to orbit the Earth or are we going to keep on drifting away to the outer edges of the solar system and beyond?'

'What's that?' said Jem. Something that looked like a salt cellar had appeared between them and the Pacific Ocean. Except now it was bigger than a salt cellar, more like a dinner plate, no, a mixing bowl, no, the wheel of a car. It was getting bigger all the time. It was coming towards them.

'That,' said Lucy, 'is a rocket the size of St Paul's Cathedral filled with fuel.'

'It's huge!'

'It's coming this way!'

'It's heading straight for us!'

'Dad! Brake!'

A wall of steel with a giant 'XV' on the side of it rose up right in front of them. It kept rising and rising as they plunged towards it. It was as though they were speeding towards a crossroads while a lorry was thundering towards them in the opposite direction. The last thing they had been expecting in space was a traffic accident.

Then it was gone.

There was black and sparkling space in front of them again.

'That was close,' sighed Dad.

'Look behind!' called Jem.

The rocket was travelling so fast that it was already back to salt-cellar size. But something had fallen off it. Or it seemed to have broken in half. The bottom half was tumbling through space.

'It's a spent fuel tank,' explained Lucy. 'They jettison the spent tank and it falls back down to Earth.'

The fuel stage spun by them. It was strange to see something the size of a factory falling like a piece of litter.

'What if it lands on top of someone?' asked Jemima.

'It won't. It will break up into a billion pea-sized pieces as it hits Earth's atmosphere.'

'That's a relief.'

'Where is the rocket going, I wonder,' said Jem.

'To the moon,' said Jeremy. 'It's a Saturn V, the biggest rocket ever built. It's part of the Apollo space programme. The Americans are planning to put a man on the moon! Father was very cross about it. He thinks it would be much better if the first person on the moon was British.'

'It was nearly four hundred feet high,' said Lucy, 'and it weighed three thousand tonnes.'

'Very odd,' said Jeremy. 'A girl knowing so much about rockets.'

'We did it in history.'

'History!? When was all this?'

'Not long after England won – or lost – the World Cup. A Saturn V rocket called Apollo 11 took men to the moon in 1969. The rocket we just saw was Apollo 15 so this must be 1971.

'Oh!' said Mum. 'I thought we were going back to our own time. How come we're in the 1970s?'

'Chronojuster still a bit sticky,' said Dad. 'We might not be in the right year, but come on – nice to be in space, eh?'

'So if the Americans really do land on the moon, what do they do there? Do they do what Father said and build a great big moon base so they can make rockets there in weightless conditions and launch them using far less fuel than you would on Earth and use them to fly to Mars?'

'Not exactly.'

'What do they do then? No. Don't tell me, don't spoil the surprise.'

'OK,' said Lucy, thinking how disappointed the Potts would be to discover that the astronauts simply collected some rocks, came home and never went back again.

'At least that means it was nice and quiet in space in 1971. Just one Apollo rocket and a few satellites – nothing else to worry about.'

'Yes,' agreed Dad. 'Hang on. What on earth is that?'

'It's nothing on Earth,' said Lucy.

Coming towards them was a huge transparent slightly wobbly globe. Like a massive soap bubble. Floating inside that bubble like a plastic Santa in a snowstorm was a vast ship.

'I've heard of spaceships,' said Jemima, 'but I

T J

never expected them to have masts. Or funnels. Or propellers. Or a deck. Or a bridge. Or an anchor. Or portholes.'

It might have been a spaceship, but its cargo was clearly of earthly origin. Strewn about the deck were the Sphinx, Stonehenge, the Taj Mahal and the Eiffel Tower. Jem and Lucy recognized the ship straight away.

'Is it aliens?' asked Jemima.

'That's not aliens,' said Lucy. 'That's Tiny Jack.'

14

Tiny Jack's personal yacht – Château Bateau – is so big that when it's out at sea it's often mistaken for an island. When it's tied up in port, passers-by take it for a small town.

'How did it get into space?' asked Jemima. 'Do you think he can see us? Is he watching us?'

'What's protecting it? It's like a giant soap bubble,' said Dad.

'It *is* a giant soap bubble,' said Jeremy. 'Father was working on a way of making burst-proof bubbles for the Navy. Before he disappeared, that is.'

'Burst-proof bubbles?' said Dad. 'What a great idea! Imagine the fun that Little Harry would have in the bath with bubbles that . . .' he tailed off, remembering that Little Harry's whereabouts were unknown.

'He designed them for underwater exploration. A sailor could get inside one and let it sink to the bottom of the ocean. Hundreds of feet below the surface he would still able to breathe. This was all top secret of course. Father would never have given it to anyone without a fight.'

Jeremy and Jemima stared down at Château Bateau, each imagining the terrible fate that must have befallen their father to make him surrender a naval secret.

'Of course, if it burst when you were at the bottom of the ocean,' said Lucy, 'you would be crushed to the size of a small pizza box by the incredible pressure of the sea. Every atom of oxygen would be squeezed out of you so that you'd end up looking like a deflated balloon. And your eyeballs—'

'Thank you, Lucy,' said Mum. 'We get the idea.'

'If the bubble bursts in space, on the other hand,' said Lucy, 'the opposite would happen. Everything that would implode under the incredible pressure of the sea would explode in the vacuum of space. Tiny Jack's head would pop like popcorn. His fingers—'

'Lucy. Please.'

'So all we need to do,' said Dad, 'is pop this bubble and Tiny Jack would be gone forever?'

'Yes,' said Jeremy, 'but so would any chance of ever finding our parents.'

'Ah.'

'Or our son,' pointed out Mum.

'But how can we get to him without bursting the bubble? You can't drive a car through a bubble without bursting it.'

'You can if the bubble is burst-proof. It will just close up around us as we pass through the membrane.'

'Wait,' said Dad. 'You're saying you think we should do that? Land on Château Bateau? On purpose?'

'Of course. It's time we sorted this Tiny chap out, don't you think? For all we know, he might be holding our parents prisoner.'

'Of course,' said Dad. He didn't say what he was really thinking – that Tiny Jack didn't seem the type to hold anyone prisoner for very long. He was much more likely to have fed them to his piranhas or his wolves or his snakes or his poisonous spiders.

'I've just figured out how Tiny Jack made those old cars race endlessly round the track,' said Lucy. 'Satnav. From up here, he can use satellites to hijack the navigation systems of all the cars. He could turn every big city into a racetrack.'

'Or a pile-up,' said Mum.

'We need a plan,' said Jem.

'Maybe we should wait until night-time,' suggested Dad.

'We're in space. There is no night-time.'

'You've probably all thought of this already,' said Jemima, 'but doesn't Tiny Jack think we're dead? He thinks he blew us up at the North Pole. Isn't it best to go and grab him now before he finds out we're alive? Then we'd have the element of surprise.'

'Jemima,' said Jeremy, 'you're absolutely right.'

'Yes,' said Dad. 'I just wish you weren't.'

Passing through the skin of a burst-proof bubble is like diving into a deep pool and finding that under the surface it's dry and you can breathe. Dad retracted the sun dome. The great car dangled high above the ship. They felt cool breeze on their faces and saw the dazzle of the glitter-ball heavens. On Earth the brightness of the stars is hidden by clouds and air and the glow of our electric lights. If you look at them from space they're almost unbearably bright. Crowds of stars twinkle and pulse so that space looks like a vast glittery animal, breathing in and out. Very few people have seen such a sight. Those who have have only seen it through the thick glass of a space helmet or through the porthole of a rocket. To see it with a soft breeze in your face, while lounging in the seat of the most beautiful car ever built, well, it is . . . distracting.

No one remembered to worry about Tiny Jack until Jemima whispered, 'I really think we should land before they spot us.'

'GA GOOO GA! GA GOOOOO GA!'

Chitty's horn was so loud and unexpected that the whole membrane of the burst-proof bubble wobbled. The starlight bopped and shimmied.

'Goodbye, element of surprise,' sighed Dad, as he tried to sneak her in to land between the pillars of Stonehenge.

'Well, this is a surprise!' A red-headed lady dressed all in red with the reddest fingernails in history stepped from under the biggest of the Stone Age arches. It was Tiny Jack's nanny. Smiling, she handed Jem a red balloon with the word 'Jem' written on it, then gave one to Jemima with 'Jemima' written on it. Jeremy and Jemima got Jeremy and Jemima balloons. 'And for the grown-ups, something a bit more grown-up.' She gave Mum, Dad and Lucy cocktails stuffed with fruit and sparklers.

'Yours is non-alcoholic, Lucy,' smiled Nanny. 'Fun can be hard to find when you're too sophisticated for balloons but too young for hard liquor.'

'We weren't a complete surprise then,' said Mum, as the sparklers in her cocktail fizzed the word 'Mum' in fiery letters. While Dad's blazed 'Dad' and Lucy's 'Lucy'.

'I'm a nanny,' smiled Nanny. 'I'm sometimes surprised. I'm never unprepared.'

She held open Chitty Chitty Bang Bang's door and they all climbed out. Or bounced out. For a moment, Jem and Jemima had the feeling that the balloons that Nanny had given them were carrying them away into the atmosphere. Then at the same time they each cried out, 'We're almost weightless!' No matter how urgent your mission, your first experience of being almost weightless is a very pleasant surprise. Mum just had to try jumping up and down on the spot. Even Jeremy couldn't help bouncing up and down on the balls of his feet a little.

The air was filled with small

floating objects – paper cups, paper plates, bird-like balls of scrunched-up wrapping paper. Heavier ones were sort of bouncing along the ground.

'Welcome to Château Bateau,' smiled Nanny. 'So good of you to come on Tiny Jack's birthday.'

'His birthday?'

'Yes. Don't worry if you've forgotten to get him a present. After all, he is the man who literally has everything. He'll just be delighted that you came to his party. It can be difficult to have a party in space. Do you know why?'

'Why?' asked Mum suspiciously.

'Because there's no atmosphere!' trilled Nanny. She giggled so much at her own joke that she floated three inches into the air. 'Well, don't let's interrupt the game of hide-and-seek. You're getting very warm!'

'We're not here to play games,' snapped Jeremy.

'What a pity – after you've done so well.' Nanny smiled. 'How was the North Pole? Come on, admit it, the North Pole part was funny.'

'We were nearly killed,' said Jemima. 'Someone blew up Big Ben!'

'No atmosphere!' said Dad. 'I get it now. That's actually quite good.'

'Thank you, Mr Tooting. And what about Tiny Jack's voices – *Big Ben to Kent, Big Ben to Kent* –

doubly hilarious, surely? He did all those voices himself. He's such a talented little darling.'

'We don't care about what voices he can do. We don't care if we're getting warmer or colder. We just want him to tell us what he did with our parents.'

'And with Little Harry,' put in Dad.

'And perhaps Tiny Jack will tell you what he did with them all . . .' said Nanny, 'if you win the game.'

She turned and walked away, her high heels pinging like bullets hitting the metal deck. It was a funny thing about the Nanny. She didn't seem to be as weightless as the rest of them. It was as if some kind of magnetism kept her stuck to the floor.

'Right,' said Mum, making a decision, 'if you can't beat them, join them. And then beat them.' Then she shouted, 'Tiny Jack! We're coming, ready or not!'

Château Bateau has acres of deck and miles of corridors. Parts of its lower levels have never been explored. No one has ever counted its staircases. How would anyone even begin to search something so big?

'We'll start at the forward end,' said Jeremy, 'and work our way systematically towards the stern.'

'But what about—' began Jem.

'Don't argue, Jem,' said Dad. 'Follow Jeremy.'

Jeremy was trying to walk briskly. This isn't easy

to do in weightless conditions. You tend to drift sideways when you're trying to go forward. The harder you try, the further you drift.

'The word today,' said Dad, 'is *try skipping instead of walking*. It seems to work.'

'But shouldn't we—'

'Jem, don't dawdle. Skip.'

They were all skipping now. Being weightless in a floating palace beneath a canopy of stars is undeniably fun. 'You know,' said Dad, 'if we weren't desperately searching for our lost loved ones, this would be a great party.'

Jem had been going to ask whether it was really such a good idea to leave Chitty Chitty Bang Bang all alone when they knew that Tiny Jack was near. After all, Tiny Jack was the world's greatest car thief. Chitty Chitty Bang Bang was the world's greatest car. She was also their only means of escape. The others were about to skip into the grove of palm trees that surrounded the Château Bateau outdoor swimming pool. If Jem took one more step, Chitty would be out of his sight. He hurried back to Chitty's side.

The outdoor pool at Château Bateau has a thrilling spiral flume and an artificial waterfall that chuckles and gurgles as it spills warm water into the heart-shaped pool. 'Goodness,' gasped Jemima. 'A space swimming pool!'

'But why is there no water?' said Mum.

'Because there's no gravity,' said Lucy. 'It's all drifted off.' She remembered the afternoons they had spent having fun here before they knew it was the headquarters of a supervillain. 'There used to be an inflatable lobster in the deep end with jugs of lemonade on it.'

'I wonder what happened to it.'

'Look up.'

There, rotating in the air above their heads, was a big purple lobster. It seemed to be looking down at them like a ragged bird of prey. Jemima shuddered.

'Don't get distracted, Jemima,' warned Jeremy, pushing onward.

There was a little brightly coloured plastic bird fastened to each tree. Suddenly every bird's eyes lit up and they all tweeted.

'What's that?' gasped Jemima, instinctively grabbing Mum's hand.

'Just the Nanny's intercom,' said Lucy.

There was another warning tweet, and then they heard Nanny saying:

'Warmer . . . you're getting warmer.'

'Oh good!' said Dad. 'The word today is *going to win this game.*'

'Of course, she is evil,' said Lucy, 'so she could be lying.'

Jem leaned against Chitty's radiator, the way he always did when he was alone with her. He liked to imagine that if he spoke to her radiator, she could hear him. Thanks to the lack of gravity, not to mention her antigravity paint, she was not quite as stuck to the ground as she normally was. Normally if Chitty Chitty Bang Bang needed a push start, you would have to get some elephants to help you. But today when Jem leaned against her she drifted off a bit and them drifted back, nuzzling his shoulder. It was harder than ever to believe that she was not a living thing.

The Zborowski Lightning twinkled in the starlight. The Lightning . . . thought Jem, there's an idea . . . Without the power of the Zborowski Lightning, Chitty Chitty Bang Bang was just an unbelievably beautiful big car. It was the Lightning that allowed her to travel in time. Just to be on the safe side, Jem unscrewed the Lightning and hid it in his pocket.

*

Beyond the palm trees that surrounded the swimming pool, Jeremy and the others came to a wide open space – a strip of black that swept in a great curve towards the bridge.

'What's this?' he asked.

'It reminds me of something,' said Dad, 'but I'm not sure what.'

Suddenly there was a roar of engines, a flash of metal and a cacophony of motor horns. A fast car was screaming towards them.

'Now I remember,' said Dad. 'It's the racetrack.'

Brakes squealed. Blue smoke streamed from the back of the car. The air filled with the sharp tang of burning rubber. The car managed to stop just in time to avoid Tooting carnage.

It was a pert white Aston Martin DB5. The slickest, chicest sports car the world has ever known. Even when one has just almost killed you, it's hard not to admire it. 'Golly,' said Jeremy. 'Look at the aerodynamic lines and the stylish headlights.'

'The word today is *British engineering at its very finest.*'

'Is this him?' said Jemima. 'Is Tiny Jack in there?'

The car didn't move. Its engine stopped. Its door opened. Jemima reached for Mum's hand but she never found it. When she saw who got out of the car, she ran. Towards the Aston Martin.

'Mummy!' cried Jemima.

'Daddy!' called Jeremy.

For stepping out of the car – one on the driver's side and one on the passenger side – were a handsome man and an elegant lady in matching polo-necked jumpers.

'Oh, Mummy! You're alive!'

'Why on earth would I not be alive?' said Mrs Mimsie Pott. 'I've always been alive.'

'What about my Little Harry?' said Mum. 'Is he alive?' But the Potts were too happy to hear Mum's worries.

'We didn't know where you were. We thought you'd crashed in supersonic Big Ben,' said Jemima.

'Not at all. We met this little chap – Tiny Jack – who brought us to this wonderful ship,' smiled Mimsie.

'We were so worried about you.'

'And we're STILL worried about Little Harry,' said Mum.

'Yes. I was worried about you children too,' said Mimsie. 'But Caractacus was absolutely certain you would find us. After all, you still had Chitty Chitty Bang Bang.'

The Commander offered Jeremy a manly handshake. 'You took good care of your sister and you found us. Well done, son.' But Jeremy hung back, looking awkward.

'I'm afraid I've let you down,' he said. 'I tried to protect your secret laboratory, but it seems this evil genius – this Tiny Jack – has stolen some of your finest inventions – the Miniaturizer, the burst-proof bubble.'

'Jeremy, don't give it another thought,' said the Commander. 'He didn't steal those things at all. I gave them to him.'

'You *gave* Tiny Jack the Miniaturizer!?' gasped Lucy. 'Are you crazy?'

'Lucy!' snapped Dad. 'This is Commander Pott. *The* Commander Pott. I'm sure he knew what he was doing. Pleased to meet you, Commander Pott.'

'Please, call me Caractacus.'

'Oh. Tooting. Tom Tooting. I've been – we've been – helping the children look for you. It's a great honour to meet you, sir.'

The Commander was staring at Dad a little bit too intensely. Dad realized he was still wearing the Commander's naval cap and a pair of binoculars. 'I brought you these,' bluffed Dad, handing them back, 'in case you needed them. We've also brought your magnificent car.'

'How is the old girl? How did she handle in space?'

'WHERE IS LITTLE HARRY?' yelled Mum.

'Little Harry?' said Mimsie. 'Oh, he's such a darling. And you know, he's always, always right. About everything.'

'Where *is* he?'

'He's with Tiny Jack. They're in the Toy Box, playing that board game. They seem to be quite obsessed with it. Still, it makes them happy.'

Leaving the Aston Martin parked on the track, Commander Pott led them past the sunloungers and up the marble steps into the living quarters. Here the floor was tiled with black and white squares so that it looked like the chequered flag in motor racing. There was a huge chandelier dangling from

the ceiling, made entirely of tree-shaped in-car air fresheners. A huge statue of St Christopher – the patron saint of motorists – stood in the stairwell. The lamps were headlights. The banisters were curling chrome bumpers.

'He really does like cars,' said Jeremy.

'Yes, he really does,' agreed the Commander. 'He's got the most astonishing collection, including his own gold-plated Paragon Panther. Strange, as I thought there was only one ever made. He even calls his Chitty Chitty Bang Bang – isn't that a coincidence?'

'That *is* Chitty Chitty Bang Bang,' said Lucy.

'But I thought you came here in Chitty Chitty Bang Bang?'

'Yes, but we seem to have crossed the Time Divide. There's only one Chitty, but it now exists in two different places at the same time.'

'Fascinating.'

Yes, thought Lucy, that is fascinating. What would happen if the two ever met?

'I wouldn't want to try it,' said Jemima, as though she had read Lucy's thoughts. 'You always get punished when you break the laws of physics.'

'Did you just read my mind?'

'No, we just think alike.'

'That's a horrible thought.'

'This Tiny Jack,' said Jemima. 'He really is tiny, isn't he?' She was looking at a framed photograph of Tiny Jack holding a Toblerone. Next to him, the bar of chocolate was the size of a ladder.

'That's actually debatable,' said Lucy.

On the first deck of Château Bateau, all the doors are bright yellow metal – like the doors of New York taxicabs. On the second deck, there are folding glass doors like the ones you might find on a bus. The Toy Box is perched on the top deck, behind the bridge. The outside is painted racing green, just like Chitty Chitty Bang Bang. Jeremy strode over and opened the door.

The Toy Box on Château Bateau is full of amazing things. The floor is paved with board games. The Monopoly board there is so big you can walk around it. The playing pieces are big enough to sit in and pedal. It has an oak chest full of real money. In one corner of the room a tank of hungry pythons slithered over each other – ready for snakes and ladders with real snakes (and real ladders).

More amazing than the extravagant toys was the view. The Toy Box has a glass roof, which was now filled with a view of the moon. It was huge and ghostly, the shadows of its mountains like some strange magical writing.

But there was something in the room that was

more amazing than the view of the moon, more amazing than a chest of money or a tank full of snakes.

'Little Harry!' shouted Mum.

Little Harry was crouched over a board game with a hammer in one hand and a dice in the other. He looked up so suddenly that he floated into the air.

'Mummy!!!!!!!!!!'

He tried to run to her. It was always amusing to see him run on his rapid, fat legs. But to see him run in weightless conditions, when each step propelled him into the air, was hilarious. Every time he rose up, he looked thrilled. Every time he landed, he looked bewildered. Thrilled – bewildered – thrilled – bewildered – thrilled – bewildered. Even if you are far from home at the mercy of a supervillain, it was hard not to laugh. Finally he crashed into Mum's legs and locked his arms around them. His own feet drifted up off the floor behind him.

'I feel we're getting warmer,' said Mum. 'Come on, everybody, we have to win this game.'

'What game?' asked Mimsie.

'Hide-and-seek. We're trying to find Tiny Jack.'

'Couldn't we just forget about Tiny Jack and go back to Basildon?' sighed Dad. But even as he said it, he knew it was impossible. Tiny Jack must be stopped, and they were the only people who could stop him.

Jem held the Zborowski Lightning up to the Earth. It hovered over England, and he pretended to make it fly down across Spain over north Africa and on to the Indian Ocean – all the places that they had flown in Chitty Chitty Bang Bang on that first adventure. It was funny to watch the little silvery biplane blotting out bigger and bigger chunks of the shrinking Earth. Was the Earth shrinking? Yes, definitely. Ten minutes ago the Lightning covered one corner of India. Now it covered the whole of India and most of the Indian Ocean. He had thought they were in orbit around the Earth but no, they were flying away from Earth, further and further into space.

From somewhere nearby he heard the clink of gravel. Something was moving behind one of the great fallen stones of Stonehenge. Quickly he shoved the Lightning into his pocket. 'Who's there?' he called. 'Lucy?'

No reply. He held his breath. He could hear someone else breathing, quick and shallow. He rooted around in his other pocket. There was nothing in there but two fifty-pence pieces and a train ticket. For the first time, he found himself wishing that Jeremy was there with him. He'd probably have been able to produce a telescope and a choice of weapons from his pockets.

'Who's there?'

Out of the shadows Lucy's voice said, 'Go away. I'm trying to contemplate all the death and destruction that engulfs the face of the Earth.'

'Lucy?' It sounded like Lucy, but how could it be her? She hadn't passed him. Why would she hide from him? He took another step closer. Now Mum's voice said, 'Jem, your sister told you to leave her alone, so leave her alone.'

It was definitely his mother's voice, but why would his mother be hiding from him? He crouched down, then pushed himself up so hard that he launched himself three metres into the air. Looking down he could see a mop of red hair, squatting behind the great stone.

A pinched little face looked up at him. 'Aaargh, you got me!' Tiny Jack leaped out from behind the stone. He floated so high he almost crashed into Jem. He seemed smaller than ever. 'I'm pretty good at voices though, eh? I can do 'em all. Listen to this: This is your dad – The word today is *I could live like this*.'

Tiny Jack did sound uncannily like Dad as he drifted back down.

'That's how I fooled you with the radio on Big Ben. Good at hiding too, eh? I've been crouched behind there for hours. I did think one of you would have found me before now. I guess that just means I'm really good at it.'

Jem remembered when the Tootings first taught Tiny Jack to play hide-and-seek, long ago in the Amazon rainforest. Of course he wasn't called Tiny Jack then. He was just a little boy called Red, having fun. Jem suddenly felt something that he never expected to feel – slightly sorry for Tiny Jack. Imagine if you just loved hide-and-seek and the only way you could get anyone to play with you was by abducting their children or their parents.

'Happy birthday,' said Jem.

'Thanks,' said Tiny Jack. 'What did you get me?' Then he saw the gleaming green chassis of Chitty Chitty Bang Bang.

'Ah, nuts!' growled Tiny Jack. 'Chitty Chitty Bang Bang. I already got one of those . . .'

'Oh. No. She's not a present,' said Jem. 'She's—'

'Wait a minute, wait a minute, wait a minute. I was told there was only one Chitty Chitty Bang Bang. NANNY!'

When he shrieked, all the little plastic birds tweeted in reply:

'Yes, sweetheart!'

'What's going on? There's another Chitty Chitty Bang Bang down here on the deck!'

'That's actually the same Chitty Chitty Bang Bang, but from a different era . . .'

Tiny Jack had already worked himself into a terrible, red-faced rage. He was furiously kicking Chitty Chitty Bang Bang's wheels.

'Ga gooo gaaaa,' wailed Chitty.

'If you hurt that car, then you'll also damage your own beautiful gold Chitty. That Chitty is the green caterpillar from which your own gold butterfly of a Chitty will emerge.'

Tiny Jack stopped kicking and shrugged at Jem. 'Just checking the tyre pressure,' he said. 'This was the biggest game of hide-and-seek of all time, and you won it! Let's go and tell everyone!'

'No,' said Jem. He'd decided now that nothing would get him to leave Chitty's side.

'Come on, you have to tell them. Especially,'

said Tiny Jack, 'Jeremy Pott. If he's anything like his daddy, he's got pockets stuffed with maps and knives and compasses, but did he beat you? No. You won. I can't wait to see his face.' Jem had to admit that it would be quite nice to see Jeremy's defeated face just for a second. Tiny Jack grabbed Jem's wrist and dragged him towards the pool. They had only made two kangaroo bounds when Jem said, 'No. Wait.' He turned back to Chitty.

She was gone. She had been there. Now she wasn't there. What had happened?

Tiny Jack shrugged as he landed next to Jem. 'Complimentary valet parking. We take care of all our visitors. Nanny has put Chitty in the car park. She'll be safe there. It's very, very secure. No one gets in or out without *my* permission.' He laughed.

He carried on laughing all the way through the palm grove, up the stairs and up to the Toy Box. He never let go of Jem's wrist. He was surprisingly strong, as though the muscles of a massive man had somehow been scrunched down into his tiny hand. Then he burst through the door of the Toy Box yelling, 'Look who won!' as he propelled Jem into the middle of the room.

'Jem?' said Mum. 'Where have you been?'

'Jem found me!' cried Tiny Jack. 'He's the champion! The hero! Across the wastes of time and space, he tracked me down. Let's give him a round of applause.'

Everyone clapped. Jem flushed. It was nice to see Dad and Jeremy applauding him, even if they were only doing so because an evil supervillain told them to.

'You have to admit,' crowed Tiny Jack, 'I totally fooled you all with that Big Ben stunt. Even that brainbox Lucy thought I was in Big Ben.'

'Big Ben is the name of the bell, not the tower,' pointed out Lucy sniffily.

'She may know the names of public buildings, but she doesn't know how to beat Tiny Jack. What shall we play next? What about Scalextric with real cars?'

'We're not here to play games,' said Mum.

'Actually I really like Scalextric,' said Dad.

'What about Destruction? That's my favourite. Look . . .'

There was a half-played game of Destruction on the table. On the board were models of the Colosseum and the Great Wall of China. Except the children knew these weren't models. 'It's easy,' said Tiny Jack. 'One defends, the other attacks. When you win, you get to destroy your opponent's property . . .' As he said this he brought a little hammer down hard on a tiny Empire State Building, reducing it to dust. The children shuddered.

'Just look at the mess you've made,' snapped Mum.

'That's the game. That's the rules!' protested Tiny Jack.

'I'm not talking about the game,' said Mum. 'I'm talking about history. You've messed up history. And geography.'

'And you made England lose the World Cup,' put in Dad, 'which is worse than both.'

'Fun, fun, fun?' explained Tiny Jack.

'Travelling in time,' said Mum, 'is like playing with Lego. It's fun while it lasts, but you have to tidy everything up when you've finished, otherwise someone will stand on one of the pieces in the dark and really hurt his foot. The Pyramids, Stonehenge, the World Cup and Basildon – you have to put them all back. We'll help you. But it has to be done. We have to put the world back the way it's supposed to be, so that life can be lived as it's supposed to be lived.'

'I say,' said the Commander, applauding. 'Excellent speech.'

The others joined in the applause. Tiny Jack wiped a tear from his eye and said, 'Mrs Tooting, you've shown me the error of my ways. I've done wrong, but now I'll put it right.'

'Well said,' said the Commander, applauding again.

'Big kiss,' said Dad, giving Mum a big kiss.

'This is so much worse than fear and chaos,' said Lucy.

'I suppose,' said Tiny Jack, 'that I should give back my unrivalled collection of amazing cars too?'

'Steady on,' said the Commander. 'There are some remarkable vehicles in that collection. Apart from that beautiful Aston Martin, he has a DeLorean that travels in time . . .'

'That never really worked,' admitted Tiny Jack.

'The very Mercedes that Mr Benz gave to his daughter Mercedes.'

'She cried when I stole it. She was only eight years old.'

'But that's far too young to have a Mercedes, even if you are a Mercedes,' said the Commander. 'He also has a car shaped like a bat.'

'It belonged to some sort of crime-fighter type. I had to tow it away as he kept chasing me.'

'He has a Beetle that was driven by the Beatles.'

'I stole it from the stage door. You see, I stole them all. It was wrong. I see that now. I'll put them all back.'

'Good boy.' Mum smiled at him.

'There's just one thing, one last little thing I'd

like to do first,' said Tiny Jack. He said this in exactly the voice that Little Harry used when he was trying to delay his bedtime. 'Just one little thing,' he repeated.

'Just one little thing,' echoed Little Harry.

'Oh, go on then,' said Mum, who never could resist Little Harry.

'I'd like to take Chitty Chitty Bang Bang to the moon.'

'To where?'

'The moon, the moon, the moon. I'd like Chitty Chitty Bang Bang to be the first car on the moon.'

There was a long pause.

Everyone looked up at the moon.

Since the dawn of time people have looked up at the moon and dreamed of walking on it. Dad first

heard about men walking on the moon when he was a little boy. Growing up, he had the impression that if some men had walked on the moon, then it would only be a matter of time before everyone could. Like most men his age, he was a disappointed astronaut.

Jeremy and Commander Pott had spent a lot of the last two years reading every newspaper report about the Space Race – the Russian rockets that had been round the dark side of the moon; the American rockets that had splashed down safely in the sea . . . How they had longed to be part of it. And now . . .

'I could take some of you with me,' suggested Tiny Jack with a shrug.

Tiny Jack was offering the Tootings and the Pott family the chance to do something that almost every family since the first family that ever lit a fire had dreamed of doing. Of course they knew that

Tiny Jack was a villain and a liar but . . . the moon.

Only Jem had the presence of mind to say, 'It's a trap.'

'We'll probably need a young chap to sit in the front and read the map,' purred Tiny Jack.

'Oh!' said Jem. 'That's me!' Even Jem could not resist the offer of a front seat on a lunar landing. 'I always read the map. I always sit in front,' he said.

'You got a map of the moon?' asked Jeremy.

'No,' admitted Jem. 'Do you?'

'Of course,' said Jeremy, pulling a little red book from his pocket. 'There's one in the back of my diary.' He flicked it open at the lunar map page.

Now that he wasn't going, it all became clear again to Jem. 'Don't be fooled,' he pleaded. 'He'll probably maroon you on the moon.'

'Jem, Jem,' said Dad. 'Don't be upset. We can't all be lunar navigators.'

The Commander cleared his throat. 'I feel I should say a word about Tiny Jack,' he said. 'Tiny Jack came to see me, all the way from the future, in his gold-plated Paragon Panther, and caused chaos at Big Ben. Apparently in the future many of my inventions – like jet packs and floating houses and edible gramophone records – are all the rage.'

'Because they're so wonderful,' put in Mimsie.

'So he thought I was just the man to help with

his scheme. He told me that in the future – which is now – there is a race to see who would be first on the moon – America or Russia. He said the first man was one thing, but wouldn't it be rather nice if Britain put the first *car* on the moon. The car of course would be Chitty Chitty Bang Bang, the finest example of British engineering the world has ever seen. I explained that we British don't have enough money to build a rocket big enough to take a car into space. He said, "But what if we did it without a rocket?" You can do a lot with a Miniaturizer, some antigravity paint and a burst-proof bubble. As we have demonstrated by taking his splendid ship into space.'

'You *shrank* yourselves?' asked Jemima. 'Mummy too?'

'We were positively microscopic for a while,' said Mimsie.

'Wasn't that incredibly dangerous?'

'Not if you read the instructions carefully and make sure you've got plenty of room around you when the effects wear off. There was a slightly embarrassing incident at the testing stage when Caractacus regained his normal size inside a pillar box.'

'What was he doing inside a pillar box?'

'Testing the theory that people could travel by

post. If they were small enough.'

'So as soon as we were safely in outer space and shipshape and normal-sized,' said the Commander, 'your mother plotted a course for the moon. Girls are so good at navigation, I find. Especially in space.'

'A map is just a big knitting pattern when you think about it,' said Mimsie modestly.

'I believe it is our patriotic duty,' said the Commander, 'to see this thing through. At least I believe it's *my* patriotic duty to try to put a British car on the moon.' The Commander stood straight. Mimsie sniffed back a tear. Dad shook the Commander firmly by the hand.

'We even brought a flag,' said Mimsie, taking a Union Jack out of her handbag. 'Tiny Jack of course wants to do it for world peace,' she added.

'Really?' said Lucy. 'I find that hard to believe.'

'America and Russia are always fighting. This silly Space Race is just another fight but in space. We thought how wonderful it would be if someone went to the moon, not for war but for fun, fun, fun.'

'That's a beautiful thought,' sighed Jemima.

The door burst open and Nanny strode into the room, her bullet heels zinging on the metal floor. 'I have a surprise for the birthday boy,' she said with a smile. She reached into her handbag and brought out a birthday cake on which hundreds of rocket-shaped candles were already blazing. There were enough candles to barbecue an ostrich. Birthday-candle heat blasted the room as she started to sing 'Happy Birthday'. First the Potts and then, reluctantly, the Tootings joined in.

'It's so kind of you all,' gushed Nanny, 'to make this such a special day for my dear little charge. A birthday on the moon! What a lucky boy.'

Dad asked Tiny Jack how old he actually was.

'A lot older than he looks,' Nanny answered for him.

'You must be quite old yourself.'

'Tom! Don't make personal remarks,' scolded Mum.

'I'm only saying she doesn't look old. But she must be old.'

'I do find that frequent time travel is very good for the skin,' preened Nanny. 'Tiny Jack does like to beat Old Father Time at his own game.' Then she started to sing 'For He's a Jolly Good Fellow', and again the others joined in. This was too much for Jem. How could anyone call Tiny Jack a jolly good fellow? 'He is not a jolly good fellow!' he yelled. 'It's all lies.'

'Jem!' gasped Dad.

'Someone's a teensy bit grumpy,' said Nanny,

'but we're not going to let that spoil our party now, are we?'

'Which part is lies?' asked the Commander.

Jem wanted to say, 'The part about jet packs and edible records catching on. No one has ever heard of these things!' But he knew how painful it would be for Commander Pott to hear that his entire life's work had been completely forgotten. So instead he said, 'It's not even his car! He stole it from us! He's Tiny Jack, the world's greatest car thief!'

'That's true,' said Dad. 'But . . . you know, the moon, Jem. I mean . . . the moon.'

'He is Tiny Jack now,' said Mum, 'but he used to be Red, the little boy who came with us to El Dorado. Maybe we should give him a chance.'

For a moment Jem almost wavered. He remembered Red's joy when he played hide-and-seek for the very first time. How he had wanted to play it forever. That was five hundred years ago now, of course, but all the same . . .

'Who would be driving Chitty to the moon?' asked Lucy.

'Well, I feel that I should go in case anything goes wrong,' said the Commander.

'Isn't it time there was a female on the moon?' asked Lucy.

'Oh, that would be so nice,' said Jemima. 'I'll go. I won't be any trouble.'

'The word today,' said Dad, 'is *it's my car*. He stole it from me. The least he can do is give me a lift.'

'It can't be you,' sneered Jeremy. 'Your fingers are too fat.'

'Jeremy, don't make personal remarks.'

'Dinosaurs!' yelled Little Harry.

'How about we play a game for it?' said the Nanny, lifting the lid of the snake tank. 'What about snakes and ladders . . . with real snakes?'

Mum thought herself pretty good when it came to snake-wrestling. Jemima had dealt with snakes during her days in South America. Everyone wanted to go to the moon so everyone said yes. They crowded around the snakes-and-ladders board, each convinced that they would win. Only Jem stepped away. High over all their heads, through the Toy Box dome, the moon loomed brighter and more mysterious than ever. Of course he wanted to go there every bit as much as the others, but how could they trust Tiny Jack? How could anyone trust Tiny Jack? And besides, if it was to be decided by a game of snakes and ladders, what was the point? Jeremy's pockets were probably stuffed with Everything a Boy Would Need for dealing with deadly snakes and wobbly ladders.

He slipped away.

The others seemed to have lost their wits. The only person he felt he could really trust was not a person at all. It was Chitty Chitty Bang Bang.

Jem crossed the deck of Château Bateau in long, unintentional bounds, heading for the car park where he hoped to find Chitty Chitty Bang Bang. Every now and then he'd bump into something in mid-air. Everything that wasn't actually nailed to the floor when the ship had left the Earth was now floating around in the air. Dressing gowns and towels, lifebelts from the pool, deckchairs and champagne buckets from the observation decks, books, magazines and the guns and bombs that Tiny Jack used to scare off intruders, all dangled in the air like strange birds.

The car park on Château Bateau is not your average pay-and-display multi-storey. It is Car Heaven. There is a fully integrated car wash that cleans each car at the entrance. Perfumed breezes waft the car dry afterwards. Each car has a room of its own, with a numbered door. The whole place has a dangerously effective security system.

Jem tiptoed in through the main door, thus activating the integrated car wash and getting soaked to the skin. Dripping, he went from door to door, peeping inside. There was the Maharajah's Rolls-Royce, its gold giving off a soft, buttery glow. Here was a DeLorean, a car whose doors opened upward like wings. Finally, in room number 23, was Chitty Chitty Bang Bang herself. When Jem slipped in through the door the great green machine seemed to move back a little nervously, the way a horse does when you enter its stall. Then he floated towards him, barging against his shoulder affectionately. Or possibly trying to push him out.

Last time Jem had visited this car park the security system had consisted of hundreds of poisonous jumping spiders. Nervously he scanned the walls and wheel arches for a glimpse of a hairy spider leg or a poisonous spider jaw. He reached into his pocket for a torch, but then remembered that he was Jem, not Jeremy, and didn't actually have a torch.

He tugged his jumper up over his face and his sleeves down over his hands to give himself the best protection he could. Then he heard the rattle of metal. A chain. Was there some kind of ferocious watchdog chained up in here? Holding his breath, Jem bent down to take a look. No. There was a chain but it wasn't fastened to a dog. It was padlocked to

Chitty's axle. She was tied up like a rogue elephant or a mad dog.

'We'll soon sort that out,' said Jem, patting her running-board. 'Where's your toolbox? We can cut this off for you.' He knew there should be a pair of wire cutters in the toolbox that was normally stashed under Chitty's front seat. Jem pulled open the back passenger door.

That's when he discovered that Tiny Jack had upgraded the security system.

Spread out on the back seat was a pile of stripy, tawny fur. It looked so inviting and warm that Jem reached out to touch it.

Then it looked up at him.

It had huge headlamp eyes. They focused on him.

It had thick, muscular shoulders. They bulked up, ready to leap.

Its jaw was flanked by a pair of gleaming, carving-knife teeth.

It opened its mouth and roared.

Ah, thought Jem, a sabre-toothed tiger.

15

In this life, each of us has his own way of fighting off pythons. The technique you choose to fight off a python says a lot about who you really are. Commander Pott for instance, used the classical, explorer's technique, which involves making yourself as big as possible by filling your lungs with air and tensing your muscles while the snake wraps itself around you, then breathing out and relaxing your muscles so that you become small enough to slip out of its coils. Then there's the direct approach of grabbing the snake behind the head and bashing it about a bit, favoured by Mum. There are those who use weapons. Jeremy for instance liked to fire his catapult at them. This is very effective. You don't even need to aim straight to get a result from doing this as the snake can see the missile coming and will try and strike at it – helpfully throwing itself in the path of flying pebbles or whatever. A hatpin is good if, like Mimsie, you wear hats with pins in. You can dazzle a snake with your make-up mirror, like Jemima. You can try to unsettle the snake by climbing up a ladder and making it rock from side to side. The corresponding floor vibrations give the snakes a funny feeling in their tummies. Since they navigate by tummy, this can completely disorientate them. They end up trying to eat draught excluders, cushions and close family friends.

Tootings and Potts all fought well and hard.

No one was eaten.

But the winner of the game of snakes and ladders with real snakes (and real ladders) by a considerable margin – was Dad.

It seemed all he had to do was wiggle his hands in a snake's face for it to become soft and cooperative. It seemed the snakes mistook Dad's chubby fingers for tiny baby snakes, and this made them go all gooey and sentimental.

Dad was going to the moon. 'And all thanks to my chubby fingers.'

'Mr Tooting is going with me to the moon!' declared Tiny Jack.

Everyone cheered.

'I also want Commander Pott and his little boy,' said Tiny Jack. 'In case she won't start and I need a push.'

'Shouldn't the composition of the crew reflect the make-up of our families more accurately?' asked Lucy.

'What?' said Tiny Jack.

'You need a girl. Namely me.'

'Oh no, no, no,' said Nanny. 'We girls are going to have a girly get-together while the boys are playing with their rockets and things.'

'I think I'm going to be sick,' said Lucy.

The first thing most people ask when they see a sabre-toothed tiger is . . . 'What on earth is the point of those huge, curving carving-knife teeth? Who needs teeth that are bigger than their mouth?'

The answer is that sabre tooth cats first arrived in the Pleistocene era – the age of supersize mammals, like mastodons, mammoths and giant elks. If you're going to eat a big dinner, you need big teeth, teeth that can slice through arteries and crunch through bones even when those bones are buried beneath mats of mammoth hair and elk muscle.

When most people see a sabre-tooth for the first time, it's on Wikipedia, or on the telly. However, if the first time you see a sabretooth, it's crouching down on the seat of your car, growling and ready to pounce, the question that springs into your mind is less likely to be 'What exactly was the evolutionary advantage of those incisors?' and more likely to be 'What am I going to do?'

Jem thought quickly. He grabbed Chitty's bodywork, pushed off and vaulted into the air. As the cat jumped, he floated clean over its head. The cat yowled in fury, then slammed against the garage door.

Jem had one advantage over the cat. Jem liked being weightless. The cat hated it. It had curled up on Chitty's seats and dug its claws into the leather just to enjoy the sensation of not floating around for a while.

The cat however had an advantage over Jem. When it slammed against the garage door, the door clicked shut. The cat was now between Jem and any means of escape.

Jem was at the back of the car. The cat was at the front. He thought that if he made like he was going to run away down the passenger side, the cat might go for him, and then he could dodge over to the driver's side.

'Here, kitty!' he teased, leaning out as far as he could.

The cat paused, trying to figure out what was going on. It raised one thick, muscular paw and slammed it against Chitty's front wheel. The spokes rattled. Chitty swung from side to side like a saloon door.

'Ga gooo ga!' she blasted.

'Oh, don't do that, Chitty,' whispered Jem. 'I'm trying to steal you in secret.'

At the sound of Chitty's Klaxon the cat did not even blink. Its eyes were fixed on the boy. The boy was the cat's favourite combination of things – edible and annoying. It could solve two problems – the boy's annoying existence and its own hunger – by sinking its two incisors into that convenient gap between the boy's top two ribs.

'Come on, kitty!' called the boy down the passenger side. Clearly the boy was planning to dodge back. Had he never watched a cat hunting? This was the oldest trick in the very old cat book. The cat actually yawned, turning its back on him.

Had it lost interest in him? thought Jem. Maybe it wasn't hungry.

Bang! The cat was suddenly on top of Chitty's bonnet, sending Chitty see-sawing up and down with the force of its landing. There was not going to be any left–right dodging about. The cat was coming straight down the middle. Down the centre of Chitty's bonnet it came. Over the windscreen it slunk. It perched on the dashboard. It sprang on to the back of the passenger seat. It was face to face with Jem now, only one bound away. Its muscles rippled.

The cat leaped. The boot! Jem whipped the boot up. Moving in weightless slow motion, the cat saw it coming. It swivelled in the air. It hit the boot with its feet and pushed off like a swimmer. It got ready to swing again.

Jem looked down into the boot. Should he climb in there? Close it after him? What was in there? The antigravity paint spray. Could that work? Jem snatched the spray. There was still paint in it. He closed the nozzle and worked the pump. The creaking of the pump intrigued the cat. It growled.

Jem levelled the nozzle. Then he slammed the boot shut. Suddenly the cat was face to face with Jem again. It unsheathed its teeth. It leaped at him teeth first.

Jem flipped the nozzle. A fine spray streamed out. Some of the weightless droplets drifted off into the air, but he was close enough and the pump was strong enough to make sure that all the cat's underbelly was splattered with the paint.

The paint clogged in the soft fur. The cat shot upward, yowling and howling, claws and jaws flashing, Catherine-wheeling round and round, its back flush with the ceiling. Jem did not speak sabretooth but he knew what all that spitting and squealing meant. It meant, Get me down get me down get me down!

While the sabretooth spat and yowled above his head, Jem rooted the wire cutters out of the toolbox. He came around the front and wedged the blades around Chitty's chain, but the links were so thick that they barely fitted between the blades of the wire cutters. No matter how hard he pushed, Jem couldn't get them to make even a nick in the metal.

'Come on, Chitty,' he coaxed, speaking into her radiator. 'You've got to help me, if I'm going to help you . . .' He leaned his back against her and pushed. The massive car rolled over the wire cutters. Their blades slipped neatly through the chain.

Chitty Chitty Bang Bang was free. And Jem was in the driving seat. He rested his hands on the steering wheel. That's when he heard the voices.

The excitable squawk of Tiny Jack . . .

The confident rumble of Commander Pott . . .

Dad's familiar tones . . .

Jeremy's excited voice . . .

They were all coming this way. What if they were coming here? What if they heard the racket the sabretooth was making? What would Tiny Jack do?

A warning light flashed up on Chitty's dashboard. A message spooled across it in thick black letters:

The Lightning. Of course! It was still in Jem's pocket. He took it out. The silver propellers caught the light and splashed sparks across the ceiling. The angry growling changed to a bewildered purr, as though the big cat had changed gear. It tried to follow the pretty lights with its eyes as the propeller sent them round and round and round, until the cat's eyes grew weary and it fell into a deep, peaceful sleep and dreamed it was lying the right way up on solid ground. Very quietly, trying not to attract the cat's attention, Jem screwed the Lightning back into place. He could make out what the others were saying by now.

Tiny Jack was showing off his cars.

'How on earth did you get such a marvellous

collection?' That was the voice of the Commander.

'They're mostly stolen. As you know, I was a car thief. Until I reformed. Started out as a car thief and worked my way up to stealing ancient monuments. But stealing cars was my first love. I mean, until I became a reformed character of course. Now I'm far more interested in . . . errrmmm . . .'

'World peace?' suggested Dad.

'That's it.'

They were coming nearer. Jem huddled down in the seat.

'How did you become a reformed character? How did you stop being a thief?'

'There was nothing left worth stealing. Sad, really. This collection of stolen cars is complete. I've got Bugatti's own Bugatti. Ferrari's own Ferrari. Winston Churchill's boyhood pedal car. And in here of course is . . . Chitty Chitty Bang Bang.' Jem held his breath. Was Tiny Jack going to open the door?

'This way, please,' said Tiny Jack.

Sweat broke out on Jem's forehead.

'Chitty's just through here, gentlemen . . .'

A door opened, but not Jem's door.

Of course! Tiny Jack wasn't interested in the dear old racing-green Chitty Chitty Bang Bang. He wanted to ride around in the gold-plated Chitty.

There was a loud roar.

'Good heavens!' That was Commander Pott again.

'The question today,' said Dad, 'is *did I just see a sabre-toothed tiger?*'

'Security system,' explained Tiny Jack. 'Some of these cars are very valuable. But I didn't want to mess up their paintwork by putting alarms on them. Or wheel clamps. So I went back in time and got some big frightening cats. I used to have poisonous spiders, but the cats are easier to feed. Now,' sang Tiny Jack, 'bring me my Chitty Chitty Bang Bang of gold.'

It gave Jem a strange feeling to think that they were looking at the very same car that Jem was sitting in, but from a different time. It gave him goosebumps. Chitty Chitty Bang Bang's steering wheel shook a little in his hand and her electrics whined briefly. Maybe she had automobile goosebumps.

'If your collection is complete –' it was Jeremy talking now – 'why is there still one space in your car park? This room is empty.'

There was an awkward pause. In his mind's eye Jem could see Tiny Jack turning even redder than usual, getting ready to explode because someone had asked him the wrong question. Then, 'Jeremy,' he said. 'Have you got the map? Jump into the front seat. Let's fly to the moon.'

The green Chitty's electrics whined again. Her steering wheel shuddered. Through the door she could hear the hand crank turning in her other self.

Chitty – she heard her engine starting up somewhere else.

Chitty – it was hitting its stride.

Bang – she was purring nicely, but there and not here.

Bang – she was moving off, while at the same time staying quite still.

Commander Caractacus Pott was piloting the golden Chitty Chitty Bang Bang, her sun dome sparkling, through the mountain passes and over the craters of the moon. Jeremy Pott perched next to his father, his knees around the gearstick. Tiny Jack sat in the passenger seat. Dad was in the back. Next to Dad on the back seat was the world's only PBPBP.* Since we first learned to look, we have looked at the shadows of the moon's mountains, imagining we can see faces or oceans in them. Everyone has seen the shadows of the mountains, hardly anyone has seen the mountains themselves.

* PBPBP – Personal Burst-Proof Bubble-Producer.

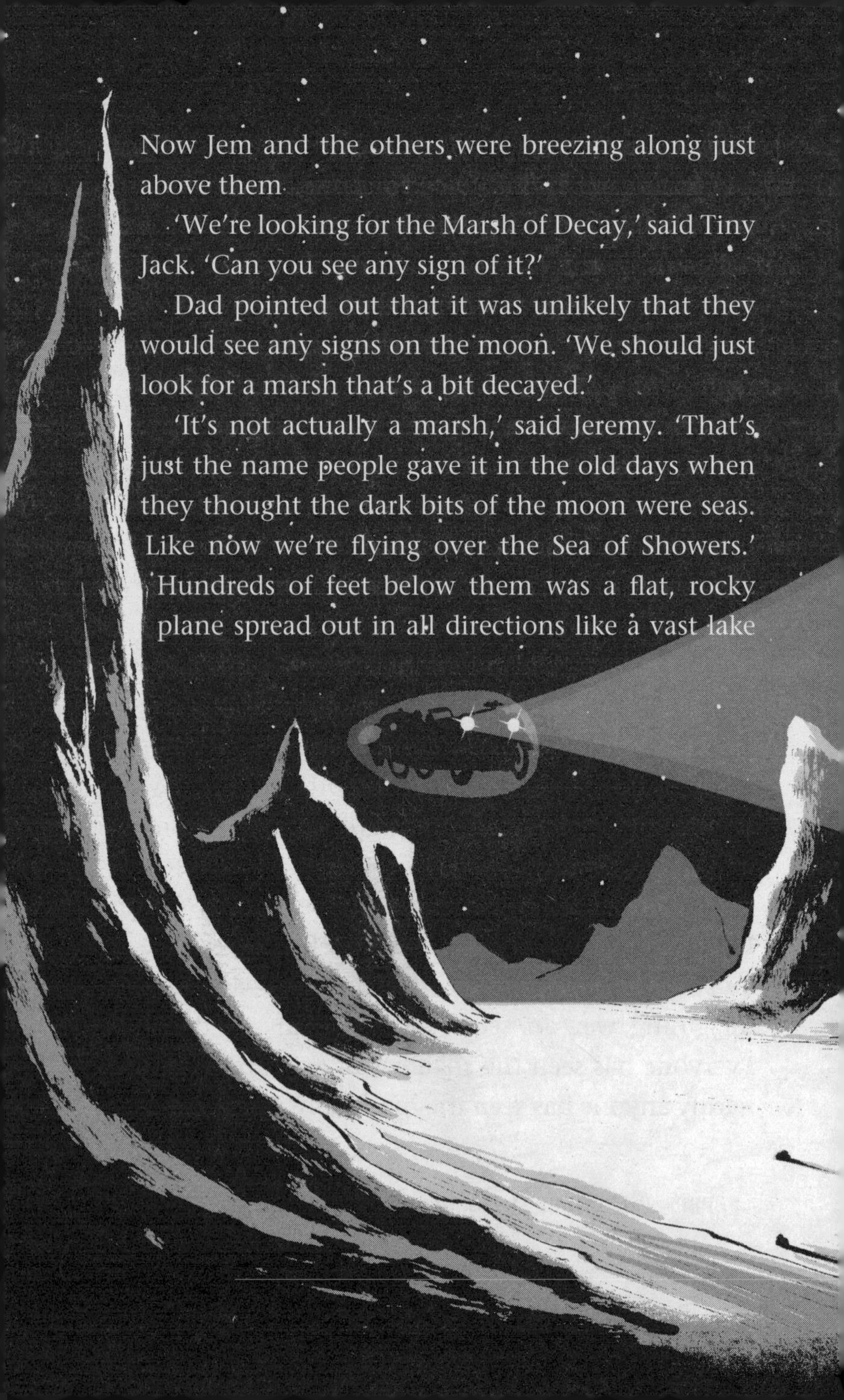

Now Jem and the others were breezing along just above them.

'We're looking for the Marsh of Decay,' said Tiny Jack. 'Can you see any sign of it?'

Dad pointed out that it was unlikely that they would see any signs on the moon. 'We should just look for a marsh that's a bit decayed.'

'It's not actually a marsh,' said Jeremy. 'That's just the name people gave it in the old days when they thought the dark bits of the moon were seas. Like now we're flying over the Sea of Showers.'

Hundreds of feet below them was a flat, rocky plane spread out in all directions like a vast lake

of melted toffee. 'It's not a sea and it's never rained here.' It wasn't until he said it that the hugeness of that thought struck him. It had never rained here, not since the beginning of time. For centuries people had looked up at this place trying to imagine what it was really like – Was it a sea? Was it a marsh? Were there creatures living there? Now he, Jeremy Pott, was seeing it close up. He knew what it was like, knew better than Galileo, better than Leonardo . . .

'Well, if it's not a marsh and it's not decayed, how are we going to know when we get there?' screeched Tiny Jack.

'Couldn't we park here and drive around for a bit?' asked Dad. 'It looks nice and flat.'

'We have to get to the Marsh of Decay . . .' said Tiny Jack, 'BECAUSE THAT'S WHERE I WANT TO GO AND THIS IS MY CAR, MY TRIP, MY IDEA AND MY FLAG SO . . . SHUT UP.'

'OK.'

'In fact, it is OK,' said Jeremy, pulling out a little diary from his pocket and opening it at the moon. 'I have a map here. Those mountains on the horizon are called the Lunar Apennines. They're the highlands of the moon. Head for those. When you see a long channel in the ground, that's the Rima Hadley rille – follow that. Carry on as far as the big crater and turn left. Then at the third crater on your right, go right and that should bring you right into the middle of the Marsh of Decay.'

Commander Pott rubbed Jeremy's hair. Dad reached over and did the same.

'ARE WE THERE YET!' shrieked Tiny Jack. 'ARE WE THERE YET? ARE WE THERE YET?'

Soon they saw the long, dark gash in the ground that was the Rima Hadley rille. Commander Pott brought Chitty closer to the ground, getting ready to land. Her great wings bulldozed the air, her mighty exhaust stormed the dust on the moon's surface around, her large wheels churned it up. She was a gale and a tornado and a hurricane all at the same time. For miles around, the dust lifted and swirled beneath her like a carpet of sparkling grey cloud.

'I CAN'T SEE ANYTHING!' shrieked Tiny Jack, 'Are we there yet? Are we there yet?'

'It'll be impossible to land if I can't see the ground,' said the Commander.

'ARE WE THERE YET?'

'I don't know. I can't see. We need to find somewhere flat to land.'

'Maybe I can help,' said Dad.

'I shouldn't think so,' said Jeremy. 'Father was in the Navy; he knows about these things.'

'Press on the brake.'

'If I stop, we'll just fall.'

'Not always. I once pressed the brake when we were thousands of feet up and Chitty stopped in mid-air. If it worked again, then we could just wait until the dust has cleared.'

'What if it didn't work?'

'We're practically weightless. So we'd land quite gently.'

The Commander pressed the brakes. Chitty

Chitty Bang Bang stopped in mid-air. Slowly the dust began to descend, settling back into its cracks and crevices. As it fell, it became thinner and more transparent. The clouds of dust became a fog of dust, then a mist of dust and then something like a tissuepaper wrapper, then finally the air was empty again and everything seemed clear and new. It's true that everything was grey, but it was a bright, shining, fresh kind of grey.

'Just over there. It's not far,' said Jeremy. 'It looks like there's something there already. Can that be right? Could it be something to do with that big rocket? Or is it just a trick of the light?'

'That's it!' whooped Tiny Jack. 'Head for that. Aim for that . . . trick of the light.'

The Commander released the brake. Silently Chitty glided in to land.

'Hurry it up,' goaded Tiny Jack, shoving himself into the Commander's lap and grabbing hold of the steering wheel. 'OK, let's go!' he said. 'This is taking too long.'

'I can't see,' complained the Commander.

'You don't need to see. I can see. I'll steer. All you have to do is work the pedals.'

'What if we need to brake suddenly?'

'We won't need to brake at all. We're in a hurry.'

Banners of moon dust fluttered and flashed

behind them as they sped across the Marsh of Decay.

'That is not a trick of the light,' said the Commander. 'That is some kind of object – a man-made object.'

The air on the moon is very clear. You can see even faraway objects in great detail. They could see every detail of the boulders that dotted the slopes of the faraway mountains and the craters that lay at their feet. They could also see that the object they were approaching was made of metal. It was held together by rivets. It stood on jointed insect-like legs of steel. It had a doorway. It had the number 15 painted on the side, and beside that the American flag.

'Oh blow!' said the Commander. 'We've been beaten to it.'

'Apollo 15!' said Dad. 'You know the Apollo landings were all on TV. This means we're going to be on TV all over the world.'

'Accelerate! Accelerate!' shouted Tiny Jack.

'Is there any point now? We might just as well enjoy the view,' said the Commander.

'I SAID ACCELERATE! THIS IS MY CAR! IF I SAY ACCELERATE THEN YOU ACCELERATE OR GET OUT! FASTER! FASTER!'

The Commander pushed on the accelerator.

The sun rose over the Lunar Apennines. Its first rays lasered into Chitty. She must have looked like a fireball speeding over the plane, her gold alight with sunshine. As they got closer to the spacecraft, Tiny Jack swung on the steering wheel so hard that he was lifted right off the Commander's knee. 'Brake! BRAKE!' he cried as Chitty spun on her back wheels, shovelling a great column of dust into the air before plunging to a halt with her back bumper to the spacecraft.

'We should go and congratulate them,' said the Commander. 'I feel that's the proper thing to do.'

'Activate the PBPBP,' snapped Tiny Jack. 'I need a big, big bubble.'

'Is that me?' said Dad. 'OK.' He pressed the red button on the PBPBP and a froth of tiny bubbles appeared in the mouth of the machine. One of the bubbles grew bigger and then bigger. One moment it was the size of a tennis ball, the next the size of a football.

'The yellow button turns on the oxygen fountain,' said the Commander, 'in case you were thinking of stepping outside.'

'We're going to walk on the moon!' said Dad, pressing the yellow button. 'The word today is *lifetime ambition fulfilled*. Hey, do you think the

Apollo astronauts will come out? Are we going to talk to real astronauts?'

'We *are* real astronauts,' said Jeremy. 'We're on the moon after all.'

'Oh yeah.' Dad smiled. 'I am an astronaut.' Liking the sound of the sentence, he added, 'I'm an astronaut,' before going on to say, 'I . . . am an astronaut.'

The bubble had now grown so big that Dad was sitting inside it. Soon it filled the whole interior of Chitty Chitty Bang Bang. They watched in wonder as it grew out through Chitty's doors and roof without bursting so that the whole car was inside the bubble. The stars danced rainbows on its round, oily surface. Soon it grew so big that it enclosed both Chitty and the Apollo landing module.

'OK, that's enough,' snapped Tiny Jack. 'Jeremy, keep the engine running. Pott, round the back and pull out the tow bar. Tooting, you get the doors with me.'

'The what?'

'OK. Let's move it.' Tiny Jack jumped out of Chitty Chitty Bang Bang and stood on the surface of the moon, protected by a Pott's Patent Burst-Proof Bubble.

Dad stepped out next. 'I'm an astronaut,' he said. 'I'm on the moon.' Over to the left he could see the round, blue Earth watching him like a child's eye. He waved to it. 'I'm an astronaut!' he called as if everyone on Earth could hear. 'And it's all thanks to my fat fingers.' He looked at his fat fingers as he waved. If they hadn't been fat, he would not have been sacked. If he had not been sacked, he would never have begun this great adventure at all. It was his fat fingers that had helped him defeat the pythons and win his place on the trip to the moon. 'The word today,' he sighed happily, 'is *fat fingers are the best*.'

'Get your fat fingers round this,' said Tiny Jack, pushing a long black crowbar into Dad's hands. 'Is the motor running? Pott, are you ready with that tow bar?'

'Yes, the tow bar is here, but I don't quite understand—'

'OK, team, let's do this.'

Tiny Jack kangaroo-hopped across the surface of the moon, to the command module. The module had a small pod on top that looked like living quarters. There was another pod underneath, lower, more boxy, sitting almost on the ground. It had a door with some kind of seal on it. Before the others had time to work out what was going on, Tiny Jack had wedged his crowbar into the seal and jemmied it off. 'Now you, Tooting. Just swing on it.'

Tiny Jack's voice was so commanding and his tone so urgent that Dad did as he said without a

thought. The door of the pod broke off and drifted slowly to the ground. A ramp slid into place.

'Nice work,' said Tiny Jack, dropping his crowbar. 'Is that engine still running, kid? It had better be.'

'Yes, but—'

'Let's keep it that way.'

He dashed inside the pod. Dad, the Commander and Jeremy looked at each other, uneasy and embarrassed. What was going on?

A few seconds later they knew. A vehicle came bouncing out of the pod. Four wheels, massive tyres, no roof, just a seat and a lot of wiring. Tiny Jack was at the driving wheel, whooping and cackling.

'That,' said Dad, accurately, 'is the moon buggy.'

'Most expensive car ever built! And here I am, stealing it.'

He drove it right up to the back of Chitty Chitty Bang Bang, where the astonished Commander Pott was waiting in a kind of trance of amazement, Chitty's tow hook in his hand. Without even looking at him, Tiny Jack took the tow hook from him and fastened it to the front of the moon buggy. He grabbed hold of Chitty's wheel arch and swung his low-gravity self in a beautiful arc, right to the driver's side door.

'Time for your moon walk, Jeremy,' he snarled,

and yanked Jeremy out of the car. He pulled Chitty's door shut behind him.

'Wait! What are you doing?' yelled Dad. 'You can't . . .'

Chitty said 'Chitty', twice; and then 'Bang Bang'. Tiny Jack slipped the car into gear. The sun dome clicked into place.

'No, no, wait . . .'

Too late.

The golden Chitty Chitty Bang Bang rolled forward, sliding out of the bubble.

She was only inches away, but as unreachable as if she had been in the heart of the sun.

Dad, Commander Tooting and Jeremy watched in despair as Chitty Chitty Bang Bang, with the NASA moon buggy behind, bumped away from them over the rocky plain, swinging from side to side as Tiny Jack divided his attention between steering and accelerating.

'We've been marooned,' said Dad, 'in a bubble on the moon.'

Across the plain, Chitty Chitty Bang Bang lurched into the air. Tiny Jack swept her into a turn that took her curving low over them, so that the whole bubble wobbled. They could see him grinning out of the window.

'The greatest feeling in the world,' he chortled to

himself, 'is leaving someone behind.'

'Five minutes ago,' said Dad, 'I was an astronaut. Now I'm a car thief.' He looked at his fat fingers as if they might offer some explanation.

A few moments later two figures appeared from behind the lunar module. They were Apollo astronauts, dressed in full spacesuits, carrying massive backpacks and wearing huge boots. They were wearing big reflective helmets so it was impossible to see their facial expressions, but Dad thought it was probably safe to say they were surprised to find two men and a little boy in shirt-sleeves waiting for them on the surface of the moon.

Slowly the astronauts inched towards them.

'We come in peace,' said Dad.

Commander Pott was carrying the Union Jack. He waggled it at them and said, 'God Save the Queen?' but had the feeling that this wasn't really helping to clarify things.

The astronauts looked inside the broken pod and saw that the moon buggy was missing. They spread out their arms as if to ask, '*What?* Where has it gone?'

'It wasn't us,' said Dad. 'A little boy did it and then ran away.'

16

'Chitty Chitty Bang Bang!' yelled Little Harry, pointing out of the Toy Box window. Jemima followed his finger and saw the beautiful car rise from the surface of the moon, her golden bodywork shining like a meteor.

'Here they come!' she cried. 'At least they're safe.' She trained her father's binoculars on the flying car.

'Daddy on the moon!' whooped Little Harry.

'Oh,' said Jemima. 'Oh dear no.'

'What?'

'Oh no.'

'Oh no what?' Lucy was getting impatient.

'Little Harry was right. They're not all aboard.'

'What? Who's missing?'

'Father is missing.'

'Oh dear.'

'And Mr Tooting.'

'No!'

'And Jeremy.'

'You mean . . . Tiny Jack is coming back alone?'

'Yes. He must have left the others behind on the moon.'

'You can't leave someone behind on the moon,' said Lucy. 'The lack of pressure would mean that they would—'

'Please, Lucy. No details,' said Mum.

'But surely he can't have left them?' said Jemima.

'Well, now that was a bit naughty,' said Nanny, who had joined them at the window. 'I will give him a bit of a talking-to about that when he gets home. Marooning guests on the moon – honestly.'

Lucy checked the binoculars. There was no doubt about it, Tiny Jack was all alone. Chitty seemed to be towing something. It looked like a shopping trolley with a satellite dish on the back.

'Oh no!' said Lucy. 'Oh no, no, no. This is all my fault.'

'Lucy, what are you talking about?'

'I was the one who told him about it. He'd never even heard of it until I mentioned it.'

'What is? What's happening?'

'Tiny Jack is the world's greatest car thief. So

why did he go to the moon on the thirtieth of July 1971?'

'He's going to make Chitty Chitty Bang Bang the first car on the moon,' said Mum.

'He's going to fly the flag for British engineering,' said Jemima.

'He's going to steal the Apollo Lunar Rover, the moon buggy, the most expensive car ever built – thirty-eight million dollars. And what made him think of it? I did. I told him all about it.'

'Thirty-eight million dollars,' chuckled Nanny, 'and it doesn't even have a car alarm. They really were asking for it.'

'I don't suppose they expected anyone would go to the bother of travelling all the way to the moon to steal a car,' said Lucy.

'Doing the unexpected is the essence of the art of the thief,' said Nanny.

'But . . .' protested Jemima, '. . . he said he was going to plant the Union Jack.'

'He told a lie. It's really very difficult to steal things if you only tell the truth. When we stole the Sphinx do you think he said, "Hello, I'm stealing the Sphinx?" No, he said, "Hello, I know just the man to repair that nose."'

'This is terrible,' said Mum. 'The Apollo moon landings were live on television. Millions of people are going to see your father steal a car. The whole world will think he's a car thief!'

'Daddy would never be an accomplice to a crime,' said Jemima. 'I'm sure he'll stop him.'

'I'm afraid he's already been an accomplice,' said Mimsie.

'What?'

'How did Tiny Jack get here? With burst-proof bubbles and antigravity paint. Your father and I have already helped him on his way.'

'And I was the one who told him about the moon buggy,' said Lucy. 'I thought I was being clever but I put the idea in his head.'

'We all helped him,' said Mum. 'If it wasn't for us, he would never have had the Diamond As Big As Your Head.'

'You've all been so helpful,' smiled Nanny, backing out of the room. 'I almost won't enjoy doing this.'

They heard a click as she locked the door behind her.

'Hey! Wait! What are you doing?' shouted Mum.

'I do apologize for the inconvenience, Mrs Tooting,' Nanny called from the other side of the door. 'You've been a true inspiration to me. Your commitment to tidying up has inspired me to do some de-cluttering of my own.'

'What are you talking about?' said Mum.

'The Toy Box,' yelled Nanny from the other side of the door, 'really is a box. It's held down by a few catches, here –' they heard the snap of a metal catch being undone – 'and here –' another snap. 'As you can hear, I've undone those catches. This sound –' clunk – 'is me strapping a small explosive charge on to the side of the box. When I detonate the charge, it will shoot the Toy Box up into space. Since there is no friction in space, the box will just keep going on and on into deeper and deeper space . . .'

'Bang!' yelled Little Harry.

'But why?'

'Tiny Jack has completed his collection, stolen the world's most expensive car. Everything else is just clutter. Get rid of the clutter. You are the clutter. Goodbye.'

'But what will become of us?' said Jemima.

'Intelligent question,' said Nanny.

'Bang Bang!' yelled Little Harry.

'In fact,' said Nanny. 'The lack of physical friction in space means that the Toy Box will keep drifting. Since you're unlikely to hit any physical object, you'll continue to drift. For Ever. And Ever. I'll be commencing countdown shortly.'

'Why do villains always talk so much when they're about to kill you?' wondered Lucy. 'Surely they must know that just gives the hero more time to come to the rescue.'

'What hero?' asked Jemima. As she said this, the glass dome above their heads shattered into a million little pieces. Thanks to weightlessness the shards of glass floated harmlessly around the room like unusually bright snow.

'Ga GOOO ga!'

The mighty radiator of the racing-green Chitty Chitty Bang Bang thrust itself through the crystal blizzard and into the room. Jem was at the wheel.

'Anyone need a lift?' he said.

'Ah,' said Jemima. '*That* hero.'

'Chitty Chitty Bang Bang,' said Harry. It was what he'd been trying to say all along.

Nanny heard the racket on the other side of the door. She scrabbled with the lock. She got the door open just in time to see Chitty Chitty Bang Bang's registration plate – GEN II – disappearing backwards through the hole in the shattered dome. When Nanny hurried into the Toy Box, Chitty flashed her headlights at her, flipped her indicators and was gone.

Nanny stormed back to the door, pulled it open and – to her astonishment – found herself looking at the Château Bateau swimming pool a hundred feet below. In reversing out through the dome, Chitty

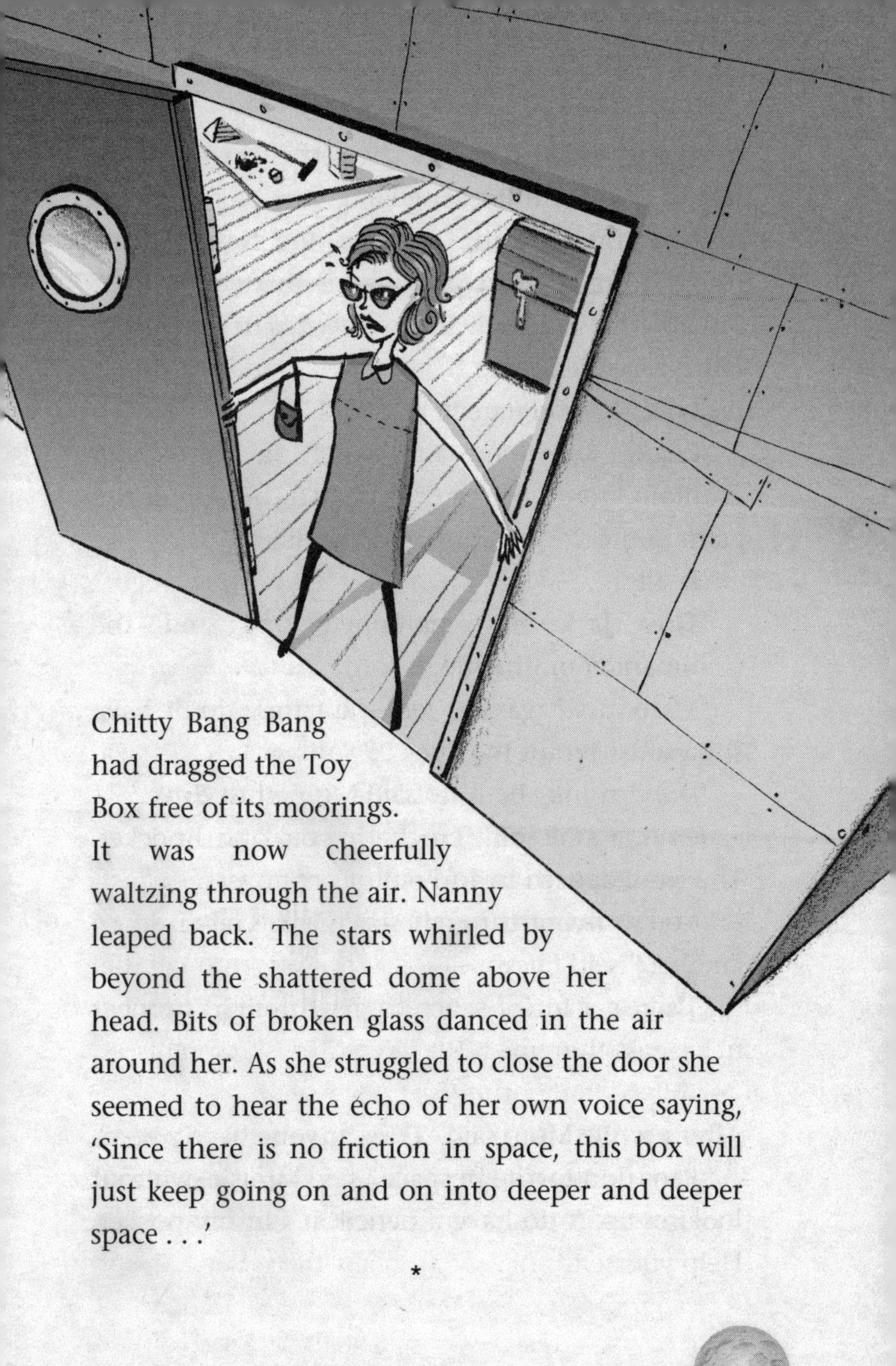

Chitty Bang Bang had dragged the Toy Box free of its moorings. It was now cheerfully waltzing through the air. Nanny leaped back. The stars whirled by beyond the shattered dome above her head. Bits of broken glass danced in the air around her. As she struggled to close the door she seemed to hear the echo of her own voice saying, 'Since there is no friction in space, this box will just keep going on and on into deeper and deeper space . . .'

*

'In theory,' said Lucy, as she settled in the front seat of Chitty Chitty Bang Bang, 'the box will keep drifting forever until, perhaps, the Nanny turns into a storm of angry protons.'

'How did you know that we needed to be rescued, Jem?' asked Jemima.

'I didn't,' said Jem. 'Chitty did.'

'Engage sun dome and switch on the oxygen fountain,' said Lucy as they neared the skin of the giant bubble. 'We're going to the moon.'

'Really?'

'Tiny Jack has marooned Dad and the Commander on the moon.'

'Marooned?' gasped Jem. 'But they don't have spacesuits! Won't they be . . .'

'Don't think about it,' said Mum. 'Just drive.'

Jemima took some crocheting out of her pocket. The wool danced in and out of her fingers.

'You're flying through space and you're doing crochet?' said Lucy.

'There's a lot of space to get through. Crochet helps pass the time.'

After a while Mum said, 'Does anyone have a pen?'

'Pens don't write in space,' said Mimsie, without looking up. 'I do have a pencil. It's in my pocket. Help yourself.'

'After we've foiled Tiny Jack,' said Mum, 'we are going to go and tidy up history. I'm making a to-do list . . .'

TO-DO LIST

1 Rescue Dad, Commander Pott and Jeremy.

2 Foil the evil genius Tiny Jack.

3 Win the World Cup for England (we would like to watch this game).

4 Return the following to their rightful places: Stonehenge
Taj Mahal
Sphinx
The Tower of London
St Pancras
Big Ben
The White House
The Acropolis

'Your list is going to be longer than that,' said Lucy, who had been scanning the Earth through Pott's Patent Superbinoculars. She passed them to Mum. 'They say you can see the Great Wall of China from space. But can you?'

Mum raised the binoculars. 'Wow!' she said. 'These are amazing. I can see roads and rivers and houses.'

'But no Great Wall. And look at Britain.'

Mum swung the binoculars across the Earth. Mountains and oceans swirled by. 'These are fabulous! That spiky bit at the top of Great Britain, that must be Scotland. Those blue bits are the lochs. Those sunny green bumps, they must be the Pennines. That must be Birmingham . . .'

'Try to find Basildon.'

Mum looked down towards London and then went very quiet. Where Basildon should be, there was nothing but a hole in the ground. 'Tiny Jack has miniaturized it to make pieces for his game of Destruction.'

Quietly, solemnly, Mum added 'Basildon' to her list.

'Let's hope we catch him,' said Jem, 'before he shrinks London or New York or Beijing.'

'Chitty Chitty Bang Bang!' whooped Little Harry.

'Yes, we're riding in Chitty Chitty Bang Bang,' agreed Mum.

'Chitty Chitty Bang Bang!' insisted Little Harry.

This time Jem remembered that Little Harry is always right. He looked where his brother was pointing. Far ahead, in space, a tiny ball of golden light was speeding towards them. It passed them in a blur – Tiny Jack on his way back to Château Bateau.

'It's Tiny Jack,' said Jem. 'In his golden Chitty.'

Chitty Chitty Bang Bang quivered. Her springs squeaked, wires twitched. Handles and switches rattled in their fittings as though she was being pulled towards some terrible magnet.

'Chitty wants to go after him,' said Jem, struggling with the wheel.

'No!' It was Jemima. She looked horrified. 'That's what I've been thinking about. Tiny Jack's golden Chitty and our own dear racing-green Chitty are both the same car but from different times. Imagine if you went into a room and you were already in there as an old woman . . .'

'That would be interesting,' said Mimsie.

'It could be disastrous,' said Jemima. 'One thing can't be two things. I have the feeling that if the two Chitties touched, something terrible would happen. Perhaps the whole universe would short-circuit or close up like a book that time has finished reading. Don't you think, Lucy?'

'You thought of all that while you were crocheting?'

'I think better when I crochet.'

'Could you show me how to do it?'

'Moon! Moon! Moon!' sang Little Harry. For there it was, hanging over them, blinding, vast and empty.

'How will we ever find them?' sighed Mimsie.

Lucy took out her jelly phone. 'We'll ring Dad,' she said. 'The jelly phones seemed to work everywhere in time and space.' The vast silence of space seemed to pivot around the tinny ringing of the phone. 'Answer, answer,' muttered Lucy.

'Hello?!'

'Dad?!'

'I'm on the moon!'

'Yes, we know. We're coming to rescue you.'

'I'm on the moon!'

'Yes. Where exactly are you?'

'Hello? Hello? I'm on the moon.'

The phone went dead. 'Never mind,' said Lucy. 'Think about it logically. They stole the moon buggy. Everyone knows that landed on the Marsh of Decay at the foot of the Lunar Apennines.'

'But how do we know what is where?' said Mimsie. 'Jem doesn't have a map. My Jeremy always has maps.'

'I don't need a map,' said Jem. 'I'm barely steering. Chitty knows the way. She's been here before, just not in this colour scheme.'

The airstream of their green Chitty Chitty Bang Bang spread a duvet of dust over the Marsh of Decay. Even through the dust they could see a flicker of bright lights ahead as though a constellation had fallen out of the sky on to the lunar surface. It was starlight playing across the dome of the burst-proof bubble. They saw as they drew nearer that the bubble was huge. The whole of the lunar module, including the empty buggy-container, sat beneath its dome.

Chitty landed herself neatly just a few metres away and Jem drove her slowly, carefully, through the membrane of the bubble.

Mum rushed to embrace Dad. Mimsie embraced the Commander and Jeremy.

'Are these the first kisses on the moon?' said Dad. 'Can someone take a picture?'

'OK, now you've spoiled the entire moon for me,' said Lucy, and climbed back into the racing-green Chitty.

She was not the only unhappy face. The two

NASA astronauts – still in their spacesuits – were sitting on the steps of the module, looking glum.

'I can see that it would be frustrating,' said Dad, 'coming all this way for a drive and finding that someone has nicked your car.'

'The moon buggy!' exclaimed Mum, taking out her paper and pencil. 'I need to add that to the list.'

'Chaps won't take off their spacesuits,' said the Commander. 'Even though we've told them they're quite safe inside the bubble.'

'Safe,' said Dad, 'but cold.'

'They think we're aliens. Or possibly Russian. They won't let us in the module.'

'They think,' said the Commander, 'that we had something to do with the theft of their lunar vehicle. Because your father jemmied the door of the pod.'

'And you hooked it up to Tiny Jack's tow bar,' said Dad.

The two NASA astronauts had got to their feet. They were staring at Chitty Chitty Bang Bang.

'Paragon Panther,' shouted the Commander, 'wrecked at Brooklands in 1922. I found her in an old garage, restored her myself in 1963.'

'And I restored her again,' said Dad, 'in . . . you know, the future. Found her . . . all over the world really. She was in pieces.'

Little Harry peered up into the astronauts' masks.

'Ice cream!' he yelled. 'Ice cream!'

'They can't hear you, inside their spacesuits,' said Dad. 'I tried writing a few things down for them, but it didn't seem to help.'

Dad's notes:

SORRY ABOUT YOUR CAR.

DO CARRY ON WITH YOUR MISSION.
DON'T MIND US.

WE'RE NOT ALIENS. WE'RE FROM BASILDON.

HAVE YOU GOT ANY FOOD?

'Oh, how I wanted a spacesuit like that when I was little,' said Dad. 'I can't believe we're standing here with real live NASA astronauts! Can we get a photograph? Lucy! Where's your jelly phone?'

Lucy was still sulking in Chitty Chitty Bang Bang, practising her crochet. Every now and then she would look up at Planet Earth. Africa was just turning into view. Lucy thought of all the places she had been in Chitty. Places that seemed so far apart but which now seemed so close together they were all the same place. Earth. She could blot the whole planet out of the picture by squinting at her thumb. For some reason, this thought bothered her.

'Come on, Lucy,' said Mum. 'When are we ever going to have another opportunity to get a photograph of our entire family on the moon?' Mum wanted both families in the photograph together so they had to persuade one of the astronauts to take the picture. The other one stood in the middle with his two thumbs up. This all took some time. Maybe looking at the smiling families through the lens of the camera phone reminded the astronaut of his home and family. For whatever reason, as Jem was cranking Chitty Chitty Bang Bang's engine, ready for the return journey, the astronaut tapped on the glass of the sun dome.

'Ice cream!' bawled Little Harry.

Jem could sort of see what he meant. The astronaut did look a bit like some kind of strange extraterrestrial ice-cream man as he reached in and handed out little silver parcels.

Oh! It turned out they were ice cream! There was a straw in one end and if you sucked hard you got a mouthful of some slightly chewy, very vanilla-ish definitely space ice cream.

'If you don't mind I'll save mine for later,' said Commander Pott.

Dad climbed into the driving seat and tried the starter motor. Nothing happened.

'Probably best if I drive,' said the Commander. 'After all, this is a kind of voyage, and I was in the Navy.'

'I just drove this car all the way to the moon from Basildon,' said Dad. 'I've really got the feel of her.'

'If you two are going to bicker,' said Mimsie, 'then I'll drive, because I've never learned how to and space is the ideal place as there's nothing to bump into.'

But no matter how hard Jem cranked the engine, Chitty Chitty Bang Bang would not start.

'Have you checked the petrol?' asked Mimsie.

The fuel gauge showed zero.

'Got the feel of her!?' snorted the Commander. 'You didn't even notice that she was thirsty.'

'Now that I come to think of it,' said Dad, 'I haven't put petrol in her since Dover. I suppose that is quite a long way.'

'It's a quarter of a million miles,' said the Commander. 'Chitty is very fuel efficient, but if you're planning to travel a quarter of a million miles, you should probably put a drop in the tank.'

Chitty Chitty Bang Bang was stuck on the moon with no petrol.

17

The golden Chitty Chitty Bang Bang was at that very moment back at Château Bateau, sliding through the membrane of the burst-proof bubble, with Tiny Jack at the wheel. She glided into land next to the Sphinx. Tiny Jack jumped out and set about unhooking the moon buggy from its moorings. As he busied himself with the clasps and hooks, he practised the great speech he had been composing in his head. 'Yes, this is it. I've excelled even my own excellence . . . no, my excellent self. I have excelled my own excellence . . . you see before you . . . no. Look at me, everyone!'

Once the buggy was unhooked, he drove it round the pool a couple of times to get the hang of it. He thought about hiding it in the palm trees for a while and then unveiling it when everyone was there to see it. But then he thought how much more brilliant it would be if everyone came down and found him already sitting on it . . . no, standing on it. Yes! He stood on the back of the moon buggy and called at the top of his voice, 'Look what I've got!!! Come and see, everyone!!!' He couldn't wait to see their faces. This must be the greatest, most amazing and daring car theft ever. 'It's my bestest ever birthday present to myself!! Come on down and bring your cameras. Hello? HELLOOOOOOO!!!'

There was no answer.

Nobody came.

'HELLOOOOOOOOOO!'

'Ga gooo ga!!!' He sounded the horn of his golden Chitty Chitty Bang Bang.

He sounded the ship's foghorn.

He set off a fire alarm.

He screamed at the top of his voice.

Every one of these tremendous noises was lost in the muffling vastness of space.

On the deck of Château Bateau, more than three hundred thousand kilometres from home, Tiny Jack was all alone.

In fact it's not really that difficult to get a car going on the moon if it's got no petrol.

'I've just remembered something,' said Jemima.

'I remembered it first,' put in Lucy.

'The lack of friction in space . . .'

'. . . means that once a thing is set in motion . . .'

'Let's say it together . . .'

The girls explained that once force is used to set an object in motion in space, it should in theory keep going. The moon dust had rubbed off most of the antigravity paint, but there was still a little left and besides there was hardly any gravity on the moon. It should be a simple matter to get her moving. All she needed was a push. Once they were up in the air, that would give them the momentum they needed to get home.

All the adults got ready to push. Even the astronauts lent a hand. Jem sat in the driving seat as he was the smallest person who could actually reach the pedals. They propelled Chitty over the rocky ground. She hit a rock. Bounced into the air and they were away. In the low-gravity conditions of the lunar surface it was easy enough to jump into the car before Jem engaged the sun dome and they slipped out of the bubble.

'Move over then,' said Dad to Jem.

'I thought we agreed it would be best if I drove,' said the Commander.

'I thought we agreed it would be best if I drove,' said Mum.

'Jem should drive,' said Lucy. 'He got us here. He can take us back. After all, he's a renowned getaway driver.'

'That's true,' agreed Jem. 'But I need someone to read the map.'

'Map of what?' asked Dad. 'We're in space.'

'The constellations. Anyone got a map of the constellations?'

Jeremy looked in his pocket. 'Yes!' he cried. 'There's one in the front of my diary.'

'Perfect. Sit up here.'

So Jem and Jeremy sat in the front, helmsman and navigator, steering that great green galleon of a car around the dark side of the moon.

'Thank you,' said Jeremy.

'What for?'

'For not saying, "I told you so," when Tiny Jack marooned us on the moon.'

In the back seat Dad and Commander Pott began discussing the finer points of Chitty Chitty Bang Bang's inner workings. There was a lot of talk about the carburettor cooling flange. The Commander was astonished to hear that Dad had originally fitted Chitty's giant engine to a VW camper van. 'I couldn't just leave a beautiful engine like that stuck up a tree, now, could I?'

'I'm surprised the van wasn't shaken to pieces.'

'People did sometimes think we were an earthquake.'

'Where did you find her body in the end?'

'On an island in the Indian Ocean.'

'Good heavens! I wonder how it got there.'

The Commander reminisced about the old garage with the tin roof where Jeremy and Jemima had first found Chitty. Dad remembered the time the people of El Dorado took Chitty Chitty Bang Bang completely to pieces and he had to put her back together again like a jigsaw. 'There were these things like atomic hairdryers.'

'Hairdryers are so useful. You can make practically anything out of a hairdryer. Those were supposed to be directable booster rockets. Never could get the blasted things to work.'

'I wired them in, but I never knew what they were for.'

'For landing safely after a space flight. You see, I always did plan to take the family for a spin in space. Just never expected it to be quite so dramatic. I was thinking of it more as a kind of scenic jaunt. That's why I put the sun dome in and the oxygen fountain.'

'Well, we can make it into a picnic now, dear,' said Mimsie. 'Look, Jemima found a bag of Crackpot's Whistling Sweets in the cologne compartment.'

'Hmmmm, thank you,' said the Commander, taking one of the musical sweets. 'You know, it was inventing these that gave me the money to restore Chitty Chitty . . . peep peep.'

'The word today,' said Dad, sucking on his sweet, 'is *tooooooooot*.' Soon everyone of them was tootling away on their Crackpot's Whistler.

Then – all together, in perfect time – they stopped, as if some great conductor had raised his baton at them. The name of that conductor was Earth. Jem and Lucy had seen the sun rise over El

Dorado and set in the Indian Ocean. They had seen it shining down on the sands of the Arabian desert and hiding below the horizon at the Pole. But they had never seen anything as beautiful as what they were seeing now. Earth was rising over the moon. A tiny blue marble with swirls of white at each Pole, it rolled up idly around the corner of the moon. From where they were sitting, Jem and Jeremy could see a hundred billion stars, but nothing in the whole shining sky was more beautiful than the little blue marble dawning over the white moon.

'That's our destination,' said Jeremy, shutting his diary. 'You really can't miss it.'

'Château Bateau first,' said Jem. 'We have to stop Tiny Jack miniaturizing any more cities.'

'Oh. Yes. Of course,' said Jeremy. 'I forgot.'

'Oh bother,' sighed Mimsie. 'I do wish we didn't have to.'

'Couldn't we go home and have a nice cup of tea first?' pleaded Dad.

'Maybe we could,' said Lucy. 'Think about it. What's the point of stopping Tiny Jack now, when he's already created so much destruction? Why don't we go back and stop him before he starts?'

'Of course!' said the Commander. 'Clever girl.'

'Cleverer still,' said Jemima, 'why doesn't Daddy

go back to the day he invented time travel and . . . not invent it.'

'Oh,' said Mum, 'that is even cleverer.'

'If he doesn't invent time travel,' said Lucy, 'then we won't be able to go home.'

'We could take you home first. Have a nice cup of tea. Then go back to 1966 in plenty of time to save the world.'

'But if you go back to 1966 and uninvent time travel,' said Jem, 'that will mean time travel never existed. That will mean we will never have had our adventures. Never met Chitty.'

'You'll wake up one morning and none of this will ever have happened,' said Jemima. 'Tiny Jack will be just another little red-haired boy. History will be safe. Not to mention geography.'

'There is one problem with that . . .' said the Commander.

'We'll wake up and not remember Chitty,' said Jem, squeezing her steering wheel as though it was a friend's warm hand. He was steering a course high over the top of the bubble, hoping that Chitty's oily black undercarriage would be more or less invisible in the darkness of space.

'There is that,' said the Commander, 'and one other thing . . .' He looked uncomfortable, as though he was about to say something he had hoped never to say.

'Of course,' said Dad. 'We can't ask a great scientist to uninvent his greatest invention.'

'It's not that,' said the Commander. 'It's only . . .'

'No,' said Mum. 'Jem, stop the car.'

'What? But what if Tiny Jack—'

'We can't just go home. We have work to do. Look down there. Look at everything he's stolen.' The lacy white towers of the Taj Mahal, a car park full of cars, ancient monuments, secret weapons – when you looked down on Tiny Jack's haul from a great height, it really was a lot of stuff.

'We did this,' said Mum. 'We found a little boy called Red. A sweet little boy with no family. All he wanted was to play. We abandoned him in New York with no one. He thought we were playing hide-and-seek. Imagine that. Imagine waiting for people to come and find you and they never come. Imagine looking for people and you never find them. He was a boy, a sweet little boy. We made him into a villain. We created Tiny Jack.'

'We gave him a lovely holiday in El Dorado,' said Dad. 'As treats go, that's quite a big one.'

'Yes, we showed him what happiness was and then we took it away from him. We showed him what a family is and then we left him alone. His life was bad and we made it worse. We took a little boy and we created a supervillain. We did it by abandoning him. I'm not going to abandon him again.'

'But he's a supervillain. You just said so! We can't go round giving lifts to supervillains.'

'You want to abandon him in space?' said Mum.

'Yes,' said Dad.

'Definitely,' said Caractacus.

'Sooner the better,' said Mimsie.

'We abandoned him once,' said Mum. 'We're not going to do it again. It's just not right.'

'Ice cream!' yelled Little Harry.

'But what about his helicopters, and his alligators, and his sabre-toothed tigers . . .' said Dad.

'Dinosaurs!' whooped Little Harry.

Mum looked at Dad and then at Commander Pott. 'When you found this car,' she said, 'what was she like?'

'She was a rusting pile of junk,' said the Commander.

'She was in pieces, scattered across the planet,' said Dad, looking across the wastes of space at the planet in question.

'But you fixed her. You fixed this car. You made it so that she could fly, go through the ocean, travel through time.'

'That's true.'

'I believe that nice little boy – Red – is still alive somewhere, even though he later turned into Tiny Jack. Just like this lovely racing-green Chitty Chitty Bang Bang still exists, even though she later turned into the flashy gold-plated Chitty.' She turned to Dad and put her hand against his cheek. 'You fixed this great car – couldn't you at least try to fix that little boy?'

An eerie silence descended over Château Bateau. Birthday balloons, streamers and paper party plates drifted – weightless and restless – in the air as though some ghosts were having a party.

Chitty Chitty Bang Bang herself seemed to be afraid as Jem brought her in to land on the racetrack. Her carburettor quivered. Her suspension squeaked nervously.

'It's because we're so near the other Chitty, which is actually the same Chitty,' said Lucy.

'Yes,' said Jemima. 'It's as though the atoms know they shouldn't be in two places at once, so they're trying to decide where they should be.'

'If they get too near to each other,' said Lucy, 'they will actually merge . . .'

'But that might cause a nuclear explosion,' added Jemima. 'We crocheted a diagram if you'd like to see.'

'Shhh,' said Jeremy. 'He surely knows that we're here. Where is he?'

Silence.

'We have to go and find him.'

'We can't leave the car. He'll steal it.'

'That's all right,' said Jem, unscrewing the Zborowski Lightning and popping it in his pocket. 'As long as we keep this with us, he can't take her away from here.'

They tiptoed through the palm grove, past the empty swimming pool and the deserted colonnades. There was a bang. They all jumped. But it was just the inflatable lobster bursting. It had collided with a broken glass and burst.

'It's possible that we'll never get out of here,' said Lucy, 'and we'll be found, centuries from now, a bunch of corpses in an empty swimming pool in space.'

Somebody laughed. No, it was the sound of water trickling.

'That's the car wash,' said Jem. He looked at the others. Was Tiny Jack in there? Should they go in after him? What if it was a sabre-toothed tiger taking a shower?

They were walking past the lovely filigree gates of the Taj Mahal now. Suddenly those gates burst into a hundred pieces. Curls and handles and locks flew about their heads like frightened birds. The air was filled with the whirr and rumble of engines and the laughter of Tiny Jack.

The moon buggy ploughed through the gates and juddered to a halt in front of them. Tiny Jack was standing on its seat, his hands on his hips, a party hat on his head, grinning down at them.

'Anyone wanna take a picture?' he said.

'Oh my goodness,' Jemima gasped. 'You just broke the Taj Mahal!'

Tiny Jack launched into the speech he had been rehearsing. 'Yes, I, Tiny Jack have excelled even my own excellence . . . You see before you . . . no, wait that's not right. Look! I stole the moon buggy!! The most expensive car ever made. While they were building it they had troops of soldiers guarding it. No one ever dreamed that someone would go all the way to the moon to steal it. Ha ha ha!!!'

'When you're this close up to it,' said Lucy, 'it looks even more like a big shopping trolley.'

'I'm the most famous, most successful, most feared, most stylish car thief in history. Now I'm going to celebrate.'

'Ice cream?' suggested Little Harry.

'I'm going to celebrate by having fun, fun, fun.'

'Oh,' said Mimsie, 'that'll be nice.'

'The most fun I ever had was in the Amazon

rainforest. I was playing with some people I trusted. All right, I should never have trusted them. But it was fun at the time.'

'Tiny Jack . . .' said Mum, 'Red—'

'DON'T CALL ME THAT NAME!!! I AM TINY JACK. I CAN DO WHAT I LIKE!!!' He calmed down a little. 'I liked the rainforest. I want the rainforest. See that continent down there . . . ?' He pointed at South America, four hundred thousand kilometres away. 'See that big dark patch at the top?'

'The Amazon rainforest,' said Lucy. 'Why *do* supervillains talk so much? Couldn't you just tell us what you're going to do?'

'I'm going to miniaturize the rainforest.'

'No, Jack, you can't do that . . .'

'Can so do that. I've got the Miniaturizer . . .' He held it up for her to see. 'And I've got this powerful transmitter . . .' He pointed to the radio dish on top of the moon buggy. 'Going to miniaturize the whole forest and use it for the Orient Express – or, as I like to call it, my train set.'

The Miniaturizer was hooked up to the moon buggy's radio telescope. Now he aimed it at South America.

'Tiny Jack! *No!*' pleaded Mum. 'The rainforest is actually the lungs of the Earth. If you destroy it, the whole planet will die.'

'Destruction,' said Tiny Jack, 'is my very favourite game.'

Jem signalled to Jeremy. Together they leaped forward, ready to overpower Tiny Jack. But Tiny Jack had slammed the moon buggy into reverse. It lurched away from them as Tiny Jack laughed. He raised the Miniaturizer. He squeezed the trigger. 'Ow!' He twitched. He winced. He looked at his own fingers in shock.

'Are you all right?' asked Mum.

'My fingers,' he gasped, 'they've gone fat!'

'Nothing wrong with fat fingers,' said Dad.

'They don't fit in the trigger. I can't pull the . . . Ow!!!' It wasn't just his fingers that were swelling up. His feet inflated like tyres.

'That,' said Lucy, 'is strangely unpleasant.'

'Ow!!!'

Now his legs were growing. His face puffed up, filled out, swelled and lengthened. His chest expanded. His shoulders broadened. Tiny Jack was growing bigger in front of their eyes.

'Make it stop!!' he wailed.

His spine telescoped. His eyes bulged.

Tiny Jack was no longer tiny.

Tiny Jack was in fact a big, big man.

'Do you mind if I film this?' asked Lucy. 'It's just so . . . unusual. Unless you're going to keep going until you explode? In which case we should find somewhere to shelter.'

'He's just getting back to his normal size,' said the Commander. 'Tiny Jack wasn't tiny until he used the Miniaturizer on himself.'

'That's why I stole it. Shrinking towns and buildings was fun. All I wanted was to stay small. I had huge furniture made so that I looked small when I sat on it. I learned a trick with mirrors that could make me look small. I thought the Miniaturizer would make me tiny forever . . .'

'No, it's effect is only temporary,' said the Commander.

'Nobody told me that! WHY DOES NOBODY TELL ME ANYTHING!!!?' wailed Tiny Jack. 'WHY CAN'T I JUST STAY TINY??? EVERYTHING WAS SO NICE WHEN I WAS SMALL. WHY IS NOTHING EVER FAIR!???'

'It was in the instructions,' said Mimsie. 'Why do men never read the instructions?'

He was redder than ever. Furious tears were boiling over from his eyes.

'Red,' whispered Mum.

'DON'T CALL ME THAT!!!! You called me that when you were pretending to be my friend . . . Everyone pretends. Even Nanny is gone!'

'The Nanny is gone? Really?' said Jem.

'We weren't pretending,' said Mum. 'We really were your friends. We had fun – real fun.'

'You left me in New York. I thought we were playing hide-and-seek. I hid behind a lamp post. I thought you would come back. No one came back. I stayed behind that lamp post all day. No one came looking for me. Only Nanny.'

'But today,' said Mum, 'we came back. We came looking for you. We're going to take you home with us.' She looked around. 'Aren't we?'

'Well,' muttered Dad, 'we could give you a lift to Earth.'

'Tiny Jack!' Little Harry sang. 'Tiny Jack,' as though it was the name of a favourite playmate.

'Do you really mean that?'

'Of course we do.'

'But,' said Tiny Jack, 'what about all my cars?'

'Good question,' admitted the Commander. 'It is a very fine collection.'

'Not wishing to worry anyone,' said Lucy, 'but if the effects of the Miniaturizer are temporary, doesn't that mean that the things that Tiny Jack miniaturized – things like Mount Everest and Basildon . . . won't they go back to their normal size?'

'Yes, of course,' said the Commander. 'That's part of the design.'

'So, for instance, Mount Everest will be here. Won't Mount Everest sort of . . . not fit? Won't it completely burst the bubble?'

'I've never tested the burst-proof bubble with an actual Himalaya,' admitted the Commander, 'but there's no reason it shouldn't work. The ship on the other hand . . .'

'Château Bateau will be crushed like a paper cup,' said Lucy. 'It will be nothing more than a pile of junk, doomed to orbit the world forever, bound by the chains of gravity to a meaningless—'

'Yes, quite,' said Mum, adding 'Everest back' to her list. 'So, Tiny Jack, are you going to come with us? Or are you going to stay on here all alone?'

'Bound by the chains of gravity,' said Lucy, 'to a meaningless cycle of lonely—'

Tiny Jack flinched when she said the word 'lonely'. He was not afraid of Mount Everest. But he was afraid of lonely.

'Can I have a lift?' he said.

18

There was a petrol pump at the side of the racetrack. Chitty Chitty Bang Bang drank thirstily, just as she would before a big race. Jem put the Zborowski Lightning back in its place, engaged the sun dome and drove Chitty over the edge of the ship and into space. She spread her wings exuberantly and, without Jem steering her, flew a deft loop around Château Bateau. When she passed the Taj Mahal, where the moon buggy was parked, they all saw her dip her wings.

'I think Chitty likes the moon buggy,' said Jemima.

'Of course she does,' said Mimsie. 'Chitty is one of a kind and so is the moon buggy.'

The massive Tiny Jack sat on the back seat, wedged between Little Harry and Jemima. His huge

head blocked out most of the rear-view mirror. So it was only when Mum suggested that Little Harry turn around and wave goodbye to the moon, that anyone saw it.

'Craft approaching aft,' said the Commander, feeling very naval all of a sudden.

'Chitty Chitty Bang Bang!' yelled Little Harry.

As always, he was right.

There, thundering after them, blazing like a comet, was the golden Chitty Chitty Bang Bang, with Nanny at the wheel.

What had happened was this:

When the Toy Box took off with the Nanny inside, it floated around, heading for deep space and the utter doom of the Nanny. All the time, Nanny held her nerve. Just as the Toy Box was about to slip off into infinity, there was a jolt. It had snagged on the left minaret of the Taj Mahal. Nanny knew this was her chance. She clambered out of the window, scrambled down the tower clinging on with her lethal red nails, and clawed her way in through one of the windows.

Down the stairs she ran and out of the broken gates, just in time to see racing-green Chitty Chitty Bang Bang fly off into space with her little charge on board.

As she ran down to the deck there was a loud rumbling followed by an ear-splitting 'pop' that seemed to rock the burst-proof bubble. The full-size 'World of Leather – Basildon' went tumbling past the bridge. Then came a terrible shaking and rattling. Everest was returning to its proper size.

Nanny grasped the situation immediately. The buildings and monuments that Tiny Jack had miniaturized for his game were returning to their normal size. This, she thought, will not be fun, fun, fun. She cranked up the engine of the golden Chitty. She flew.

Racing-green Chitty Chitty Bang Bang flew like never before. She angled her wings, swooping into terrifying dives, thrilling rolls, impossible climbs. She seemed to be dancing with excitement.

'She's never gone so fast,' said Jem.

'She never could resist a race.' Jeremy said with a grin.

But Jem knew that she was not racing for fun. She was running in fear. He could feel her rivets shivering, her carburettor pounding. On her tail was the only car in the universe that could compete with Chitty Chitty Bang Bang. That car was golden Chitty Chitty Bang Bang.

19

Racing-green Chitty Chitty Bang Bang hurtled through space, every wire and rivet straining, like a hunted deer. She tried to shake the other car off her trail by every trick she knew.

The golden Chitty Chitty Bang Bang was not fooled.

When green Chitty tried to confuse her pursuer with thrilling rolls, her pursuer did the same.

She tried to outrun her other self on impossible climbs, but her other self followed her. Both streaked ever closer to the Earth.

Ahead of them a faint glow encircled the Earth. The Earth too has a burst-proof bubble to protect it. It's called the atmosphere. As they got nearer, Chitty flashed up this message:

'What does that mean?' asked Jem.

said Chitty, adding,

Earth's atmosphere is a layer of gases that churns around the planet, like water flowing over a stone. If you want to come back into the atmosphere, you have to make sure your spacecraft – or a space car – hits it at just the right angle. Too steep and you will end up as a blazing fireball plunging to your doom. Too shallow and – just like a stone skimming the water – you will bounce off into infinite space where you will keep accelerating until you turn into a bunch of photons.

Jem didn't understand this. Nor did his dad, or his mum or Little Harry, or Mimsie or the Pott children. Even the Commander knew nothing about the physics of re-entry. Jem just saw that boiling bubble of breathable gas and thought, Right. He accelerated, he raised the wings to take Chitty into a dive and *SMACK* – the great green car bellyflopped on to the top of the atmosphere and spun off into space. Chitty flashed her headlights, revved her engine, sounded her Klaxon, but what good could any of that do? They were drifting towards infinity. They could already feel Chitty picking up speed as she slid through the frictionless wastes of space. There was no turning round now. There was no braking. There was no escape.

Suddenly she lurched backwards. Her passengers were hurled forward in their seats. Jem's head hammered into the glass of the sun dome. It was as though someone had lassoed Chitty and was now dragging her backwards. Bumper first, she plunged back into the Earth's atmosphere.

'Now do you see why seat belts are important?' said Dad, as they tore through the clouds and winds.

'What's going on?' shrieked Tiny Jack.

The answer to his question was that Nanny had got the angle of approach exactly right. Golden Chitty had slipped in through the top of the atmosphere as if she was slipping under a duvet. So great was the power of the strange molecular attraction between the golden Chitty and the green that once the golden Chitty got through, she pulled the green Chitty after her.

Now they tumbled through the upper air. They fell so fast that Jem and the others were pushed down into their seats. Jem pushed his arms forward, trying to reach the steering wheel. It was like swimming through marshmallow. As his hands grabbed the wheel, a mechanical arm popped out of the dashboard and shoved a wine gum into his mouth. 'Thanks,' said Jem, as thousands of metres below a city spread out beneath them.

'Where are we?'

The dome of St Paul's ballooned beneath them. The Houses of Parliament glittered beside the river.

'London!' whooped Jemima. 'We're going to crash-land on London!'

'Slow down!'

'How!? We're in free fall!'

'Parachutes?'

'Haven't got any!'

'Of course!' exclaimed Dad, clicking his fingers. 'The directional booster engines! We're saved!'

'Tragically I never finished them,' said the Commander. 'They don't work. So we're not saved.'

'Have a bit of faith.'

'Not to be rude, but what would you know about . . .' began the Commander. But Dad had already reached over and flicked the switch. There was a whirring sound under the floor – the sound

of a row of small atomic hairdryers shifting into place. They fired up. They shot great plumes of hot air down at the ground. Chitty hovered, bounced and then began to lower herself gently out of the sky.

They drifted over the Thames, losing height all the time. Chitty swung north of the river, over the City. 'Careful!' cried Mum as Nelson's Column rose up in front of them. Nelson himself stood nonchalantly leaning on his sword, staring Chitty straight in the headlamps, not in the least bit bothered that his hat seemed to be made entirely of bird poo. Jem twitched away from him and they circled down into Trafalgar Square and landed next to one of the fountains.

'That was one bumpy landing,' said Tiny Jack.

'The antigravity paint doesn't work as well as I thought it would,' said the Commander.

'It burned off on re-entry,' explained Lucy.

'Ga GOOO ga!' exclaimed Chitty, as though she was glad to be back on Earth.

Flocks of panicky pigeons exploded around them at the sound of her Klaxon. But they were the only sign of life.

'At least we're on Earth again,' said Dad as Chitty lowered her sun dome.

There was a terrible splash. Nelson's head,

complete with his bird-poo hat, smacked into the fountain.

'More tidying up to do,' muttered Mum, adding, 'Put Nelson's head back on his statue' to her to-do list. Jem looked up and saw a twenty-three-litre racing car ploughing down towards them. Nanny. He spun Chitty once around the fountains to confuse her golden self and then roared off down Piccadilly. Around Hyde Park Corner she thundered, up Park Lane, down Oxford Street, a right turn down Regent Street and across Trafalgar Square again, heading east this time, parallel to the river, always with that other Chitty blazing gold behind them.

The Nanny was not a great driver. At the corner of the Mall she smashed through a red phone box. As she raced the wrong way around Hyde Park Corner she ricocheted off a red pillar box.

'Can't we somehow tell her that if she catches up with us, it will possibly be the end of the universe?' asked Mimsie. 'I'm sure if we put it to her politely, she would understand.'

'Fun, fun, fun,' whooped Tiny Jack.

'The Destruction of the Universe isn't something she would want to miss,' said Lucy.

Along the Strand, Nanny chased them. When Jem drove straight into the river and Chitty ploughed across the water to Southwark, she kept after them, smashing another pillar box as she came.

'If only London knew,' mused Lucy, looking towards the City and the Bank of England, 'that if we slowed down just a little, the entire city – maybe the whole universe – would fold up like a Monopoly board being put back in its box.'

'I hate Monopoly,' said Jemima.

'So do I!' said Lucy.

'We've got so much in common,' said Jemima sweetly.

'For instance we're both most likely going to die any minute now. Do you actually have a plan, Jem?' asked Lucy. 'Or are we just going to keep the universe going by speeding around the outskirts of London forever?'

'No,' said Jem as he hit the deserted M20 and raced into Kent.

'No we're not speeding around forever or no you haven't got a plan?'

'Oh, I've got a plan,' smiled Jem. He swung north on the A229, went straight across the traffic island and took a right at the lights. Nanny was still on his tail. He pressed his foot on the accelerator but he didn't need to. From somewhere deep within her engine, Chitty found a new burst of speed. Her bonnet seemed to stretch forward like an athlete crossing the finish line.

'This stretch of road is strangely familiar,' said Mum, though the countryside around them was nothing but a green blur.

There were no signposts, but if you knew where to look there was one lying in the grass at the side of the road.

'Jem! Careful! This is—'

'I know.'

They were speeding towards Bucklewing Corner – the slipperiest and most unpredictable bend in the world.

'Please don't crash, Jem,' said Mum, clutching her to-do list. 'We've made such a mess of the world. I want to fix it all.'

But Jem knew the bend was coming. He pulled out into the middle of the road, leaving lots of space on the inside. He slammed on the brakes. Chitty seemed to understand the plan. She slowed right down, as if graciously standing back to let her other self through a door.

When drivers try to break the world speed record – driving cars that go at five or six hundred miles an hour – they sometimes try to step out of the car when it's still doing sixty miles an hour, because sixty miles an hour feels just like stopped after you've been doing six hundred. Something similar must have happened to that lovely racing-green Chitty Chitty Bang Bang, because although she thought she had slowed right down and was now ambling through the bend, she was in fact still going very fast. Far too fast for the bend.

'Look out!' screamed Jem as branches clawed the windscreen and twigs scratched his eyes.

'No!' bawled Dad as Chitty Chitty Bang Bang sailed over Bucklewing Scrap and Salvage.

'Stay calm, everyone,' ordered the Commander as sparks flew and glass shattered.

'Fun, fun . . .' whooped Tiny Jack, delirious with excitement, but before he could finish his whoop he was knocked out cold by an oncoming branch.

'Dinosaurs!' yelled Little Harry as a great golden bolt of a bonnet slammed right into the back bumper. The last thing Jem saw was the number plate GEN II flying through the air. The last thing he heard was Little Harry's happy yell: 'Dinosaurs!'

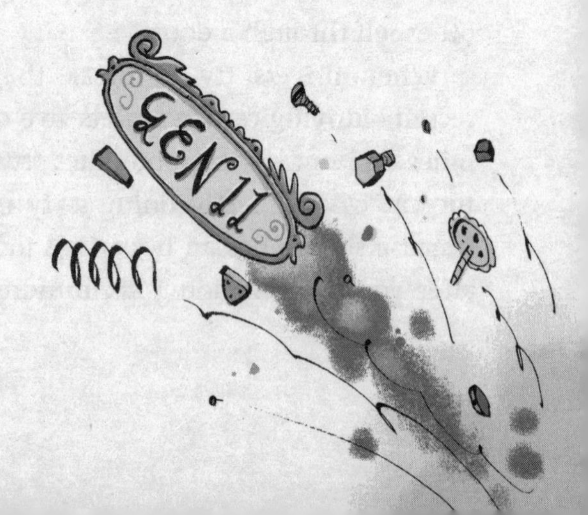

20

Little Harry is always right.

Imagine seeing every photograph of yourself that has ever been taken, all at the same time. This is how it felt to Jem. He could see himself staring up at a tyrannosaurus as its nostril twitched and its eye swivelled.

Here he was with his hands covered in oil, helping his dad sort out the nuts and bolts of a camper van on a hot summer pavement in Zborowski Terrace.

There he was running after that camper van as it tumbled off a cliff.

Here he was ducking bullets in New York.

There he was trying not to let his friends see that he was actually vaguely interested in his geography lesson.

There he was walking on the moon.

He saw himself whispering into the seemingly smiling radiator of Chitty Chitty Bang Bang.

He saw every place he'd been to, every adventure he'd ever experienced with Chitty, all in the same moment.

Is this it? he thought. *Is this my life flashing before my eyes?*

But he saw other pictures too, pictures that he wasn't in.

Here was Chitty Chitty Bang Bang crossing the line in record-breaking first place at the Brooklands Lightning Handicap 1922. Here she was going completely crazy as she smashed into the timekeeper's shed.

Here was the Count breathing on her bonnet and polishing it with his handkerchief.

Here was her original owner, Count Zborowski, climbing from the wreckage.

Here was the inside of a shed full of spider's webs

and empty paint tins. He somehow knew that this was where Chitty had waited – broken – for years, for the Pott family to find her.

Here she was on a sandbank in the English Channel with a picnic of cold sausages, jam-puffs, home-made lemonade and Crackpot's whistling sweets.

There she was parked outside Monsieur Bon Bon's famous 'Fooj' shop in Calais.

He saw the Earth rushing towards her far too fast – France, Spain, Africa, the Indian Ocean . . .

Somehow the life of Chitty Chitty Bang Bang was flashing before his eyes along with his own.

Finally there were branches rushing towards him, twigs snapping in his face, strange bird calls sounding all around, dinner-plate butterflies folding and unfolding their wings as they moved through the wet air incredibly slowly, a bubbling chorus of frogs, a howling of monkeys . . . Hang on, this wasn't Bucklewing Scrap and Salvage. Where was this?

He looked around. He scratched his head. 'Did someone fiddle with the Chronojuster?' he said.

'Are we dead?' asked Jeremy. 'Is this heaven?'

'Can't be,' said Lucy. 'Tiny Jack is here.'

The huge, lumbering bewildered figure of Tiny Jack had come to and was standing next to Dad, scratching his head. 'Is this fun?' he asked. Then, 'Ow!' he said, looking down at his feet.

'What is it? A python?' asked Mum, who was always ready for a bit of python fighting.

'No.' He bent down. There was one long, spiky red stiletto. He had stepped on the heel. The insole was smouldering. It was all that was left of the Nanny.

'Shhhh.' Tiny Jack was distracted by something that was coming towards them through the trees. A little boy with red hair just like his own. The boy didn't seem to notice them at first. He was running, calling over his shoulder, 'If you want me, you're going to have to come and find me!'

'Shhhhh,' said Tiny Jack again, as if he had just spotted the rarest and shyest animal on Earth. 'That's me. I remember this day . . .'

From somewhere in the distance Mum heard herself calling, 'Red! We're going! You have to come now!'

'You're just saying that to trick me!' squealed the little boy, laughing. 'If you want me, come and find me!'

'I know this day,' said Tiny Jack. 'When I was small, I was playing hide-and-seek in the forest. I was really happy. You called me. I went and we all got into Chitty Chitty Bang Bang and you took me away from here. I thought we were going on a little trip. But you took me away and I never came back. I never saw this place again. I was never happy again.'

Mum heard long-ago Dad call through the trees one more time: 'Red! Come now or we will go without you!'

They could see the little boy now, hesitating through the trees. In a minute he would run to Chitty Chitty Bang Bang and fly away to New York and a life of crime.

This is it, thought Mum. This is where it all went wrong for Red. This is the moment that Tiny Jack began. If we can fix this moment, then we won't end up abandoning him in New York. If we can fix this moment, then all the bad things that happened – the Himalaya-stealing, the Basildon-shrinking, the Nelson-decapitating, the World Cup-losing – will never have happened. If we repair this moment, we can repair Tiny Jack.

Through the trees, she heard the boy call, 'OK, OK, I'm coming.'

'No! Don't!'

The boy looked round. He was amazed to see Mum standing there in the forest clearing with all the other Tootings and Potts – people he'd never seen in his life.

'Don't go. Stay where you are. Play in the forest,' said Mum.

'But you just told me to hurry up!' complained the little boy. 'I'm confused now. And how are you here when you were over there a second ago?'

'I was wrong to tell you to leave,' said Mum. 'I should have let you stay here and play. You'd like that, wouldn't you?'

'Who's that?' asked Red, looking curiously at Tiny Jack – his own much older and bigger self. 'Do I know you?'

'Not yet,' said Mum. 'Red, would you like to stay here forever?'

'I'll say, ma'am.'

'But if we had to go? What if we had to leave you here? Wouldn't you be lonely?'

'Lonely? In El Dorado? Where everyone knows everyone? And everyone wants to play?'

'Go on then, you stay here and play. No, wait . . .'

He stopped.

'Red, what have you got under your shirt?'

Shamefaced, he undid his shirt. They blinked. Glinting fiercely in the shafts of jungle sunlight was a diamond as big as his head.

'You have to put that back, OK? No more stealing.'

'Really? But I love stealing.'

'OK. You can steal it, for a little while – as long as you put it back after you. Now go. Hide. Have fun, fun, fun. Play the game that never ends.'

'Thanks!' sang Red, and ran off.

'Wait!' called Tiny Jack. He ran after his younger self.

'No! Don't do that!' called Lucy.

But Tiny Jack had already caught up with Red. Red put out his hand to him. 'Come on!' he cried.

'Don't touch!' pleaded Jem.

But too late. Tiny Jack had taken his own younger self by the hand.

The moment their fingers touched, the forest shrank. Suddenly it was one picture among thousands again.

Pictures of New York, El Dorado, the North Pole, the Pyramids. Earth rushing up to meet them. France, Africa, the Indian Ocean and –

bang – a picture of a ball slamming into the back of the net.

Jem and Lucy were standing on the terraces at Wembley in 1966, jumping up and down with joy as England scored a third goal in extra time. Dad was hugging Mum.

When she saw this, Lucy stopped jumping up and down. 'No goal,' she snarled, 'no matter how beautiful or historic, can justify that kind of behaviour. Please stop hugging.'

Dad let Mum go. 'We're going to miss the next goal,' he said.

Mimsie Pott shot him an inquisitive look. 'There's another goal?'

'Any minute now. And this time the ball goes right over the line.'

Some people were on the pitch. They thought it was all over. Then a brilliant ball from Geoff Hurst set the back of the net billowing. And it was all over. England had won the World Cup. The stadium erupted.

After the game they strolled down the streets of Wembley to where they somehow knew that racing-green Chitty Chitty Bang Bang was parked.

Dad patted her bonnet. 'Very nice of you to let us see the World Cup Final, Chitty,' he said.

Jem twirled the little propeller of the Zborowski Lightning.

'Will you come back with us for tea?' asked Mimsie.

'Thank you, but I think that really would be pushing the laws of physics to the limit,' said Mum. 'I think you should give us a lift home and then take Chitty back to your own time.'

All the Tootings knew what this meant. They would probably never see Chitty Chitty Bang Bang again.

The Commander took the wheel but then thought better of it. 'It's probably best if you drive her,' he said to Dad.

'Thanks,' said Dad. He took his time adjusting his seat, relishing the smell of the wood and the leather. Jem took his time turning the crank, listening for that moment when Chitty's engine sparked to life. But soon enough they were driving out along Great Central Way and through the second half of the twentieth century, heading for Basildon and the present.

'It's nice to see World of Leather back to its old self,' said Mum as they breezed past the trading estate. 'And the central reservation is in immaculate condition.'

They drew up outside their own old house. There was a car in the drive. Not a fabulous fully restored Paragon Panther, but a car just like any other car.

Four wheels. An engine. Some seats. The kind of car that could take you to work or to school or on holiday. Then bring you home again. Though it did have a super de-icer, satnav, and four-wheel drive.

'There's our old car,' said Dad. 'We've come back in time to before I lost my job. I'm still working for Tiny Parts for Big Machines. Will you come in for a nice cup of tea?'

'Thank you, but I think that really would be pushing the laws of physics to the limit,' said Mimsie with a smile.

'So this is the future,' said the Commander, looking up and down the terraced street. 'It's not quite what I expected.'

'Yes, you should go now,' said Dad. 'Don't look at the future, it'll spoil the surprise.'

'Righty-ho.' He climbed into the driver's seat while the Tootings and the Potts started saying their goodbyes.

'We think,' said Mum, 'that when you get home you should uninvent Chitty Chitty Bang Bang. At least not Chitty, but her Chronojuster. Travelling in time is too dangerous.'

'I agree,' said the Commander, 'but—'

'Wait,' said Lucy, 'if you do that – if you go back into the past and uninvent the time machine – then when I wake up tomorrow morning, I'll still be at school and Dad will still be at work and we'll just be some people who live in Zborowski Terrace.'

'Yes,' said the Commander, 'though Zborowski Terrace does seem like a very nice terrace.'

'But . . .'

'The truth is,' admitted the Commander, 'I didn't invent the Chronojuster. There was always an ebony handle on the dashboard. When I tried it, we found ourselves sailing in South America. It's not an invention. It's magic. Chitty Chitty Bang Bang is not a masterpiece of British engineering. She's a masterpiece of magic.'

'I knew that!' cried Jem. The others looked at him. He just shrugged. 'I mean . . . nothing.'

Dad could see that Commander Pott was disappointed by the way the future had turned out. 'Never mind,' he said, placing his hand on the Commander's shoulder. 'At least England will win the World Cup after all. And you can fly Big Ben around to celebrate the victory.'

'I think it might be wiser to leave Big Ben on the ground this time,' said Mimsie. 'But we could have a nice family picnic.'

'In space? Just once around the planet in Chitty Chitty Bang Bang. In low orbit,' said the Commander. 'Nothing too fancy.'

'Could we ask you a favour?' said Dad. 'There's

a 1966 split-screen VW camper van in your secret laboratory.'

'A foreign car! In my laboratory?!'

'Yes. Only . . . she's sort of precious to us.'

'I see.'

Dad whispered, 'I call her Sneezy. You could call her that too if you liked.'

'I'd rather not.'

'If you could take care of her . . . make sure that Bucklewing's doesn't crush her. It would be nice to see her again . . . one day.'

Jem crouched down in front of Chitty's wide, warm radiator. 'Goodbye,' he whispered.

'Goodbye,' said Jeremy, who had come to crank up her engine. 'Been nice knowing you.' They shook hands. Then Jeremy bent down and wedged the compass out of the sole of his shoe. 'Take this,' he said. 'Can't see how you've managed so long without one.'

'Thank you,' said Jem.

Chitty Chitty Bang Bang never said goodbye.

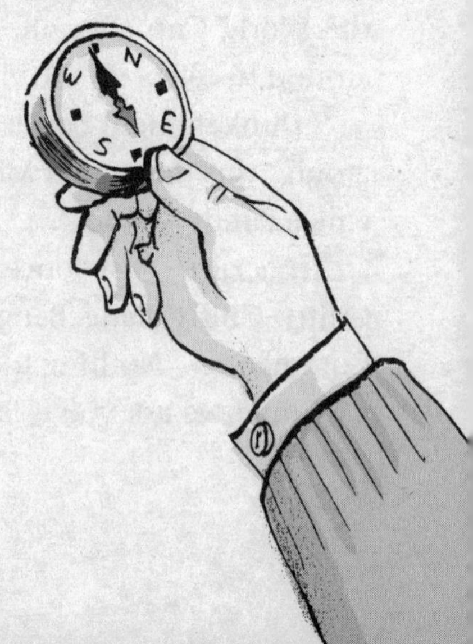

Not Quite the End

That night they got a takeaway. As they were about to eat it, there was a knock on the door. A smiley young man with a plastic name card round his neck shook hands with Dad. 'Mr Tooting?' he said. 'I'm from Tiny Parts for Big Machines.'

'Oh yes,' said Dad, thinking, I know what's coming next – he's going to sack me and take the car.

'The company has just amalgamated with another company called Average-Sized Parts for Colossal Machines. We're looking for an engineer with fat fingers. Would you like to come and join us? Nine to five. Five weeks' holiday a year and a company car.'

Dad wanted to say, 'I've been to the moon, you know. And beheld the lost city of El Dorado, not to mention landed a flying car on top of the Eiffel Tower and had a run-in with a Tyrannosaurus rex, but he didn't say any of those things. He just said, 'Oh, thanks a lot. That would be nice.'

'I'm afraid it would mean a move to Kent. Average-Sized Parts for Colossal Machines is based near a place called Bucklewing Corner.'

Dad looked at the others. 'I think we could cope with Kent,' he said.

When she was just settling down under her black duvet Lucy heard a knock on her door. Jem came in and sat on the end of her bed with Dad's punctuality map of the world on his knee.

'Re-entry,' he said.

'What?'

'I always wondered how the parts of Chitty Chitty Bang Bang were scattered so far across the world. Bodywork in the Indian Ocean, headlamps on the Eiffel Tower, wheels in the Sahara Desert . . .' He pointed to those places on the map. He remembered seeing them from space. And in Chitty's memories.

'You're saying Chitty went into space but Commander Pott got the angle of re-entry wrong . . .'

'Chitty Chitty Bang Bang broke into pieces in the

upper atmosphere. And the pieces were scattered all over the world.'

'And the Pott family . . .' said Lucy, but her voice trailed off.

'That's why none of the Commander's fabulous inventions caught on. The whole Pott family was wiped out.'

'The last thing they said to Dad is that they were going to have a low-orbit picnic to celebrate the World Cup.' Lucy bit her lip. She looked at the map.

'So when we wake up in the morning,' Jem sighed, 'none of this will ever have happened.'

Chitty Chitty Bang Bang Says Goodbye

'Jem! You're going to be late for school!'

'I know.' Jem hurried to the front door, pulled it open and then stepped back. Banks of cloud rolled by beneath his feet.

'The house went up in the night!' called Mum. 'You'll need your antigravity shoes.'

The house always floated into the air on cloudy days, so that it could catch the sunlight.

'There's no bread,' called Mum. 'Do you mind old gramophone records for lunch?'

'No, that's fine. Can I have a Count Basie one? They're sort of fruity.'

'There you go.' She gave him a kiss and waved him off.

But that lunchtime he couldn't bring himself to eat the gramophone record, so he bought a packet of Doritos and listened to the music instead. What was it about that music? It was nice enough – bouncy and unpredictable – but that wasn't it. The music seemed to remind him of something – something wonderful that he had somehow lost.

He got the feeling again that evening when he was playing with his brother, Little Harry, in Bucklewing Gardens – the beautiful aerial play-park near their house. Here you could hire jet packs and go for races around the treetops. Or bounce around the green in burst-proof bubbles.

That evening, as Lucy and Jem chased Little Harry around the turreted towers of Bucklewing House, they saw a small crowd of people gathered on the gravel path outside the main entrance. Something made Jem drop down to see what was happening.

They were gathered around a strange machine. Its bodywork was glossy racing green. It had wheels with flashing silver spokes.

'What is it?' asked Jem of the man who was standing with his hand on the strange metal grille at the front. Under the grille was a panel with the letters 'GEN II' written on it.

'Piece of junk that belonged to my father,' said the man, whose name was Hornblower Bucklewing XI.

'It's obviously a car,' said Lucy. 'You must have heard of cars.'

'I've heard of them. I've seen pictures in books. But I never saw one so big and so beautiful,' said Jem.

'No. Nor me. It reminds me of something.'

'Me too. But I can't think what.'

There was a tiny metal aeroplane on top of the grille. Jem had an overwhelming urge to flick its propellers. He did. They spun around.

'Do I have any bids?' The auctioneer was Hornblower Bucklewing XI. There was only one car for sale.

'Does it actually work?' said a man with a moustache.

'Absolutely in full running order, thanks to my good friend Professor Tuk-Tuk here . . .' He pointed to a skinny man with a beard who was wearing shorts. 'The professor came all the way from the Indian Ocean when he heard about this item.' The professor was leaning on a strange blue vehicle. It looked like a shed on wheels. It had a glass windscreen that was split down the middle so that, when the sunlight glittered on it, it looked like a pair of twinkling eyes. Written along one of its side panels was the slogan 'There is no such thing as rubbish'.

'Ice cream!' yelled Little Harry.

'Shh. In a minute,' scolded Jem. 'I want to see what happens.'

'Am I bid five pounds?'

'Five pounds,' said a rather dashing elderly gentleman in a tweed jacket with a twinkle in his eye.

'Ten pounds,' said another man in an oily overall.

'Is there any petrol in it?' asked someone else, and the bidding continued.

'Shall we try to buy it?' said Jem. 'I've got some birthday money. I don't know why – I don't know where we'll put it – but I really want it.'

'Her. It's not an it, it's a her.'

'Yes, it is. How did you know that?'

Lucy was about to say, 'Yes, let's buy her.' Then something made her look at the old man with the moustache and the twinkle in his eye.

'Jem, I really want her too. But I think that man wants her even more.'

'Sold!' said Hornblower Bucklewing XI. 'To the man in the lovely tweed coat. Name, sir?'

'Zborowski,' said the man. 'Louis Zborowski the Third.'

Hornblower Bucklewing took the money from him and helped him into the seat.

'I say,' said Count Zborowski to Jem, 'would you mind awfully cranking the engine for me?'

He handed Jem the hand crank. Somehow Jem knew exactly how to slide it on to its sprocket and wind it round until the engine sparked to life. The little crowd applauded him.

'Where's Little Harry!' asked Lucy.

'Ice cream!' called Little Harry. He was in the back of the car with his hand down the seat. Lucy pulled him out just as Count Zborowski pressed the starter motor. In Little Harry's hand was a small silver foil packet marked 'Space ice cream'.

Little Harry is always right.

Jem pulled the hand crank off its sprocket. Something made him whisper 'Goodbye' into the huge car's radiator. But the car didn't say goodbye back. Of course it didn't. It was just a car.

The gravel crunched under its great tyres as the car moved away.

'Ga gooo ga!' bellowed its enormous Klaxon as it picked up speed. Count Zborowski waved over his shoulder.

Like sunlight suddenly warming your bare skin, Jem was filled with a strange sense that the lovely world he lived in – with its floating houses, its jet packs, its antigravity shoes – was somehow a present from this big old smelly petrol-guzzling machine.

Then everyone gasped. Some people began to applaud. Up in the air, children stopped playing and hovered, amazed. The great big green machine had spread a pair of huge wings. It trundled forward

into the air and flew. It flew over the trees, banked around towards the house. They could still see the driver waving.

The exhaust was belching smoke. The car dipped and curved. What was it doing?

It was writing something, spelling something out in puffs and wisps of exhaust. G . . . it began . . . O . . . it continued . . . O . . .

They watched as the dying sun coloured the smoke red and the letters rolled out across the evening . . .

Goodbye, it said, Goodbye, Jem.

Goodbye . . .

Goodbye . . .

Goodbye.

LOG BOOK

VEHICLE	CHITTY CHITTY BANG BANG
REGISTRATION NO.	GEN II
BUILT BY	BLIGH BROTHERS OF CANTERBURY – COACHMAKERS OF DISTINCTION FOR COUNT LOUIS ZBOROWSKI OF HIGHAM PARK
ENGINE	6 CYLINDER, 300 HORSEPOWER MAYBACH AERO
BRAKES	WHO NEEDS THEM?

28 MARCH 1921

WON BROOKLANDS SHORT HANDICAP AT A SPEED OF 100.75 MPH! HUZZAH FOR US!

COUNT ZBOROWSKI

Clive Gallop

Canterbury City Council

Canterbury City Council respectfully requests that the car Chitty Chitty Bang Bang be forbidden from driving in the city as the noise of her engine disturbs the peace.

WHITSUN HOLIDAY 1922. JOLLY QUICK LAP AT BROOKLANDS – 113MPH!! SADLY CHITTY LOST A TYRE, WENT MAD WITH RAGE ABOUT SOMETHING, AND CHARGED THROUGH THE TIMING-HUT, VERY FAST, BACKWARDS! DEUCE OF A CRASH. CHOPPED OFF THREE OF MR. CHAMBERLAIN'S FINGERS.

TOP SECRET

VENEZUEL

1961 – Caractacus and Jeremy Pott hereby declare that we shall restore the rusting wreck of a car we found in a shed near Brooklands to her former glory.

August Bank Holiday 1964. Jolly nice picnic on Goodwin Sands. Boiled eggs. Cold sausages. Jam puffs. How did we get our car into the middle of the English Channel? She flew! Jemima Pott.

NOVEMBER – TERRIFIC TRIP TO SAHARA DESERT. DROVE INTO THE HEART OF THE DESERT, BUILT A HUGE SANDCASTLE. CAME HOME.

COUNT ZBOROWSKI

TOP SECRET

RECEIPT

2012 Received by Bucklewing Scrap and Salvage £50.00 in return for an old engine.

WITH THANKS

1966 – We hereby grant Special Permission for Chitty Chitty Bang Bang to Park at Wembley During Final.

THE WORD OF THE DAY WAS . . . 'ADVENTURE'

Author's Note

Stories are like cars. If you fill up the tank, pack a good picnic and just keep going, they can take you to amazing, unexpected places. But they can also get stuck in traffic, or run out of petrol and – if you're not careful – crash.

Then you need to call the emergency services.

My emergency services are my wonderful editors – Polly Nolan and Sarah Dudman. When I crashed, they came and towed me to their magical garage and straightened out the bumps. When my battery went flat they gave me a jump start. When my tyres burst they blew them up again. Once I got lost in the fog and Sarah came and blew it away and handed me a map. When I drove straight into a wall, they patiently spread all the damaged nuts and bolts and springs and screws out on the pavement and reminded me where they all went.

Thank you, dear Fleming family, for lending me your beautiful, magical car. I hope I wasn't rough with her and I'm sure she will live to fly another day. Because Professor Tuk-Tuk is right – everything and everyone can be repaired. It's only when you drive off the edge of the cliff that you discover you can fly.

My friend and collaborator Joe Berger is a wonderful co-pilot. Whenever I was stuck for an idea I would think: What would Joe like to draw? His pictures look so good that I bet when the government see them they immediately decide that Big Ben should be moved to the North Pole.

My family are always my inspiration and my help. My wife Denise is – like Little Harry – always right, always ahead of the game. But I would like to thank Heloise and Xavier especially this time. They have been the very best passengers a driver could have. They stayed awake and interested through all three journeys. They spotted all the best parking places, all the danger signs and all the passing wonders. During some particularly difficult days they took over picnic duties. Thank you, thank you.

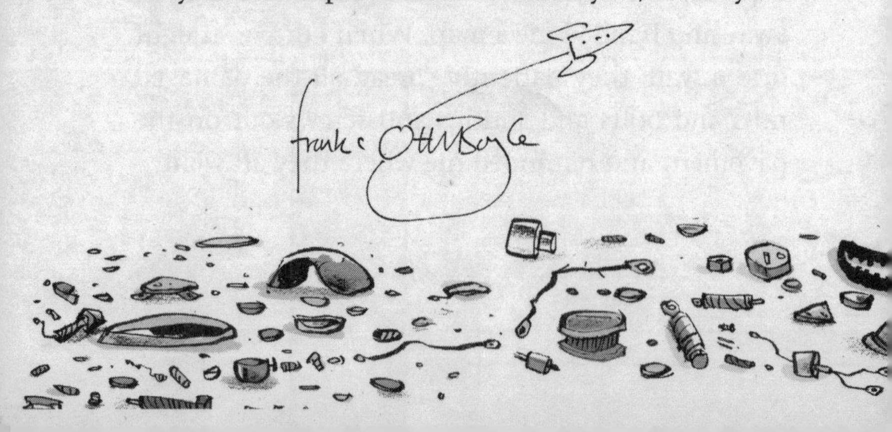